Stampede!

"The horses!" Samantha cried. "Something's wrong with the horses!"

Now Tad recognized the sound of whinnying. He and the others ran into the building. Inside, the horses where rearing and pawing the air in their stalls. Their eyes were wild with fear. A chill filled the stable.

Tad stood frozen in the doorway. There, in the middle of the stable was the ghost of Red Clarkson, a look of hatred on his face.

Completely wild now, the horses tore loose almost all at once. With terrified neighs and a pounding of hooves, the horses broke down the dry and rotted wood of their stalls and charged for the stable door—straight toward the students!

Books by Lynn Beach

Phantom Valley: The Evil One
Phantom Valley: The Dark
Phantom Valley: Scream of the Cat
Phantom Valley: Stranger in the Mirror
Phantom Valley: The Spell
Phantom Valley: Dead Man's Secret

Available from MINSTREL Books

Phantom Valley™

Dead Man's Secret

LYNN BEACH

A MINSTREL® BOOK

PUBLISHED BY POCKET BOOKS

New York   London   Toronto   Sydney   Tokyo   Singapore

This book is a work of fiction. Names, characters, places, and inci-
dents are either the product of the author's imagination or are used
fictitiously. Any resemblance to actual events or locales or persons,
living or dead, is entirely coincidental.

A MINSTREL PAPERBACK *ORIGINAL*

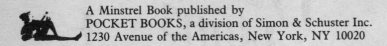

A Minstrel Book published by
POCKET BOOKS, a division of Simon & Schuster Inc.
1230 Avenue of the Americas, New York, NY 10020

ISBN: 0-671-75924-8

First Minstrel Books printing August 1992

10 9 8 7 6 5 4 3 2 1

A MINSTREL BOOK and colophon are registered trademarks
of Simon & Schuster Inc.

Printed in the U.S.A.

Chapter 1

"I hope we're going to get some wood soon." Samantha Vance looked up from the circle of rocks she'd set up. "Otherwise we'll never get a fire going in time to eat before midnight."

Tad Miller staggered up to her with a load of scrub wood he had just gathered. "Will this help?" he asked, dropping the wood and running a hand through his short blond hair.

"It's a start." Sam pushed back her long, thick auburn hair, her green eyes staring into the distance. "I wish the other guys would hurry up."

Tad watched as Sam carefully piled the small pieces of wood in a mound before stacking the larger pieces around and over it. Back home in San Francisco he'd often made a fire in the fireplace, but he had never built a campfire in the middle of a desert. He was glad Sam hadn't asked him for help. She'd see that he was a real tenderfoot.

This was Tad's first year at Chilleen Academy. His whole reason for coming to study at the boarding school was that it had the flavor of the Old West. After years of catching every western movie and reading every book about the frontier, Tad had jumped at the chance to live and learn in a western setting. He had to admit, though, he had a lot to learn about riding and camping. Still, he'd been excited when he was accepted as one of six students to go on Chilleen's annual autumn trail ride. Luckily it was still warm this time of the year in the desert.

"Here's enough wood to last all week." Randy Moser gave them a wide grin as he dropped a big load of tree branches down beside Sam.

Jane Trent, Jeff Dearborn, and Monica Case, the other three kids on the trail ride, came into camp and added wood to the pile. The wood was dry, and within minutes Sam had a huge blaze going.

"I'm starving," said Jeff Dearborn, who was blond and had a tendency to be chubby.

"You'll have to wait a little," said Mr. Taylor, coming back from the rope line where he'd been checking the horses. "Campfire cooking takes longer than microwave dinners."

Tad smiled. Mr. Taylor was one of his favorite teachers at the Chilleen Academy. He taught history, as well as running the combination camp-out and history field trip that had brought him and six students to Aramaca Canyon.

Mr. Taylor set a wire grate on four stones at the edges of the fire and put a kettle of water on to boil. Sam and Tad began peeling carrots, while Randy and Jane mixed the batter for cornbread. Monica and Jeff browned meat for their stew.

"When are we going to see the ghost town?" asked Jane Trent, her red curls bobbing as she spoke.

"Tomorrow," said Mr. Taylor.

"How far is it from here?" Tad asked, his blue eyes full of curiosity.

"It's just over this next ridge," said Sam, pointing toward a nearby rocky rise. "Can't we take a quick look while supper's cooking?"

Sam had been excited all day, talking about Kittredge, the ghost town they would be exploring. Tad wondered why it was so important to her.

"We had quite a day getting this far from Chilleen," Mr. Taylor said. "The sun is going down soon, and you know how quickly it gets dark in the desert. We'll set out for Kittredge in the morning."

"When I was little," said Jane, "I believed that a ghost town was where ghosts lived."

The other students laughed, but Tad saw that two kids didn't join in. One was Monica Case, Chilleen Academy's most talented gymnast and one of Mr. Taylor's top history students.

The other was Sam. "Ghosts aren't something to

laugh about in Phantom Valley," she said. "My family has lived around here for a long time. All my relatives have strange stories to tell."

Tad noticed that Sam's usually cheerful face was very serious.

"I've read some of the stories in the school library," said Monica. "Kittredge is supposed to be a ghost town with real ghosts. People have seen herds of cattle just disappear. They've seen phantom hangings. Some have even seen ghostly gunfights."

"That must be Red Clarkson and Johnny Bodine," said Tad. Everyone turned to him. "I've read a lot about the Old West. There are lots of stories about Kittredge, even if it isn't as famous as Tombstone or Dodge City."

Mr. Taylor nodded as he stirred the vegetables in the pot on the fire. "Yes, the town had its own famous outlaw. His name was Johnny Bodine."

"Wasn't he a train robber too?" asked Jeff.

"That's right," said Mr. Taylor. "He started out rustling horses and cattle, but went on to rob trains. He was popular with the small ranchers, though, because he'd help them out when they needed it."

"Sort of like Robin Hood with a six-gun," Jeff said.

Mr. Taylor nodded. "He was famous for only wounding people when they drew on him. He could have had twenty notches on his gun, but he never killed—until his last train robbery. That was when he single-handedly held up the Cannonball, the fastest train on the Western Central Railroad. The story goes that he was getting away with a gold shipment worth thousands of dollars. Then, for no reason at all, he shot old Zeb Frobisher, the railroad clerk who worked in the mail car."

Monica spoke up. "Frobisher didn't have a gun. Bodine killed him in cold blood. Lots of people in Kittredge knew and liked Frobisher. After word of the murder got out, everybody turned against Johnny Bodine. In the end the marshal got him."

"I read about that too," Tad said. "Marshal Red Clarkson had a showdown with Johnny and beat him to the draw. Clarkson just wounded Johnny, so they had to have a trial. Bodine was found guilty and hanged. To the very end, Bodine said he was nowhere near that train. But there were lots of witnesses who identified him as the robber, even with his mask on."

Mr. Taylor nodded, obviously pleased. "Seems like we have some real experts on Kittredge and its history," he said. "We should have an interesting time in town tomorrow."

"My uncle was traveling out this way, and he saw something really scary near Kittredge," said Randy, whose family used to live nearby. "It might have been at this very site," he said, and grinned. "He was camping alone when a cowboy dressed all in black came riding up to the fire. When the cowboy took off his hat, he didn't have a head!"

"Ewww!" cried Jane.

"Not only that," Randy went on, "his hat was full of blood."

"Tell me more," said Jeff with a laugh. "Next you'll say he threw the blood at your uncle."

"It really happened," Randy insisted.

"Sure," said Jane, rolling her eyes. "Sure it did. That reminds me of something my best friend's father told me." She began telling her ghost story.

As Jane spoke, Tad's mind wandered. It wasn't that he was bored. He liked scary stories as much as anyone. He was just more excited about the next day's visit to Kittredge. He'd be on the same street that Johnny Bodine and Red Clarkson had walked—where they'd had their final showdown.

"Oh-oh," Mr. Taylor's voice cut into the scary stories. "Who brought this last load of wood? It's all wet. We can't put it on the fire."

"Probably Tad," Randy answered, laughing. "He may have read a lot about the Old West, but he's not used to living out here."

"My wood went on first," said Tad. He hated when the guys kidded him for being from the city.

"Tad's right." Sam stuck up for him. "Come on," she said to Tad. "We'll go get some more wood."

"Just make sure he doesn't pick up any snakes, thinking they're sticks," Jeff said, elbowing Randy.

Mr. Taylor called after them. "Be quick about it," he said. "It's getting dark, and our dinner's almost ready."

"We promise," said Sam. Tad followed her away

from the circle of firelight. The sun was just sinking below the mountains, and the sky was glowing pink, orange, and purple. The high desert air was turning chilly.

"Thanks for speaking up for me," Tad said. Sam didn't say anything as she led the way up the ridge, passing clumps of trees and brush. "Where are we going?" Tad finally asked.

"I want to take a look at Kittredge," Sam said.

"Wait a minute," said Tad. "Mr. Taylor—"

"Just *look* at it," said Sam, "not explore. We'll be able to see the town from the top of the ridge."

Tad followed her up, picking up fallen branches as they walked. When he caught up to her, she was staring down at the deserted town.

Kittredge was set in a valley. On the outskirts of the town was a train station. Rusted-over railroad tracks stretched away from it. A dirt road made up the town's main street. It was lined with deserted shops and houses. All the buildings were made of wood. From that distance the town looked to Tad as if it were sleeping—as if it were a movie set.

"I can't wait till we go down there tomorrow," said Sam. "I've lived around here my whole life, but I've never been to Kittredge. It's too far to ride a horse from where I grew up."

"It's getting dark," said Tad. He picked up his load of wood. "Will this be enough?"

"We'll pick up some more on the way back," Sam

said. Just then an ice-cold wind blasted up the ridge. Tad was quickly chilled. The wind swirled around furiously, filling the air with dust.

"What's going on?" Tad asked nervously.

"Look! There's a train on those tracks!" Sam exclaimed. "But how can there be—they're all rusted!"

The train tracks that ran perpendicular to Kittredge swept in a great curve through a dip in the ridge. Suddenly a blinding flash lit up the darkening sky, and the train slammed to a stop.

"An explosion on the tracks!" yelled Sam. Her voice echoed twice in the canyon.

Tad remained rooted to the spot. He couldn't take his eyes off the train that had mysteriously appeared.

He watched as a figure on horseback rode up to one of the boxcars. The rider jumped inside, then immediately came back out, forcing another man to carry a box and tie it onto his horse's saddle. The rider remounted, stared down at the other man, and shot him pointblank. The man from the train sank to the ground and lay there very still.

"Johnny Bodine," Tad said in a low, hoarse voice.

Samantha's eyes widened. "What did you say?" she whispered back, almost afraid to break the spell.

"It's like Johnny Bodine's last robbery," Tad whispered. "He stole the money from the Cannonball, then shot Zeb Frobisher, the man from the mail car."

He stared as the mounted horseman seemed to soar up the ridge—right at them. *Nobody can ride that fast,* Tad thought. *It's impossible.*

The rider continued toward them. The dusk grew darker, and the cold whistling wind continued to blow. "Get down!" Tad shouted. He dropped the wood and pushed Sam out of the way. It was too late for him to jump aside. The horse cleared the ridge—and jumped right over him!

His own gasp was the only sound Tad heard. There was no thunder of hooves, no creak of saddle leather, no sigh of breath from the horse.

The rider disappeared in an even greater gust of wind. Tad blinked against the flying dirt. He thought he saw the rider drop something.

The wind died down as suddenly as it had blown up. Tad looked down. For a second he thought there was nothing there at all.

Then he saw it, something lying on the toe of his boot.

Chapter 2

TAD felt a sudden chill run up his back. A yellow bandanna lay on the toe of his dusty boot. He carefully picked it up to examine it. It was decorated with black designs.

"Where'd that come from?" asked Sam, her voice shaking.

"I'm not sure," said Tad, "but I thought I saw it fall from the man who leaped over me."

"I don't believe this!" Sam cried. "Where did he go?" She was shivering, and Tad knew it wasn't from the cold.

"I don't know," Tad admitted. His own heart was beating so fast, he could hardly breathe. One second the dark rider had been right on top of them. In the next, he had disappeared.

"Maybe we just imagined it," Sam said.

"How could both of us imagine the same thing?" said Tad. "You told me yourself there was a train down there. I know we didn't hear anything, but we both saw that train. And we both saw an explosion."

He stared at the tracks below. By now it was so dark, he could hardly make them out, but he could see there was no train there, and no body. In fact, there was nothing at all. Just weed-covered railroad tracks.

"A train can't just disappear," said Sam. "Unless— maybe Mr. Taylor was right." She gripped Tad's hand, hard. "Maybe what we saw were ghosts!"

Tad had been thinking the same thing. "Maybe," he said. "Except I don't believe in ghosts." He took a deep breath, remembering something his mother always said: "Seeing is believing." "No," he insisted, "I don't believe in ghosts."

"I never did," Sam said. "But what else could it be?"

Before Tad could come up with an answer, something large and black swooped down at their heads. They both ducked as it flew by.

"What's that?" shrieked Sam.

Tad looked up. "It's a bat out hunting," he said, trying to sound calmer than he felt. "Its shadow passed over us." He took a deep breath. "Maybe that's what we saw down there, just a passing shadow of some kind."

"That train—those people—were only *shadows?*" said Sam.

"It must have been," said Tad, trying to talk himself

into the idea. "After all, it was dark, and not so easy to see. Maybe a cloud passed by casting a shadow, and our eyes played tricks. We'd been listening to ghost stories—our imaginations could have run away with us."

He took another deep breath. "That's a lot easier to believe than a whole ghost train, complete with a robber."

"What about that?" Sam asked, pointing to the yellow bandanna Tad still held in his hand. "That's real."

"I know," Tad said, puzzled.

Sam jumped on his words. "Then you *don't* believe he was a shadow."

"I don't know what to believe," Tad admitted. "But I know I want to get out of here." He stuffed the bandanna into his back pocket and gathered up the wood he'd dropped. Sam quickly collected an armful of sticks for herself. Together they hiked down from the ridge.

As they saw the cheery campfire on the slight rise, the night didn't seem so scary. He could hear the excited voices of the other students. From the laughter, Tad guessed they were still telling ghost stories.

"Tad! Samantha!" Mr. Taylor called, waving them over. "I was beginning to get worried about you."

Sam hurried to set down her load of firewood. "You won't believe it," she said. "While we were up on the ridge, we saw a train robbery down on the old tracks."

"Wait a minute," Randy said in disbelief. "Those tracks haven't been used in years."

"Well, we both saw a train on them," Sam insisted.

"A man rode up and robbed a boxcar. He shot some-one. Then he rode right up to us—and disappeared—leaping over our heads."

Jeff and Jane burst out laughing, but Monica's eyes widened in fear. Randy kept arguing with Sam. Tad wished she hadn't told them what happened.

"That's a good one." Jane said. "Did you and Tad make up this ghost story while you were getting wood?"

"This isn't some silly story!" Sam insisted. "It really happened to us. Tell them, Tad."

He nodded. "I don't know how it could be. But we both saw it."

Mr. Taylor asked them both to tell their stories. "Give us every detail," he said, sounding very serious.

Sam and Tad did their best, each adding little touches. "Do you think we just imagined the whole thing?" Sam asked when they finished.

"Of course not," said Randy, sounding sarcastic. "I think you *made up* the whole thing."

Mr. Taylor surprised Tad by motioning for quiet.

"All I can say," their teacher said after a moment, "is what I told you earlier. Strange things have been known to happen in Phantom Valley. And Kittredge has been the site of some of the strangest."

Dinner was chuck-wagon stew and skillet cornbread. Tad had three helpings. He thought he had never tasted anything so delicious in his life.

Later, lying in his sleeping bag and staring up at the

sparkling stars in the black sky, he couldn't stop thinking about the scene he and Sam had "seen" by the railroad tracks. Had it really happened? Or had they just imagined it?

Then Tad remembered the bandanna he'd picked up. He pulled it out of the pocket of his jeans.

Could a real bandanna fall off a ghost? he wondered. Maybe it had been left on the ridge by a hiker. The wind could have blown it to him.

But then why had it turned up just as the dark rider had galloped by? Again he felt a shiver move up his spine. *It's just a bandanna,* he told himself. *Just an ordinary bandanna.*

As if to prove it to himself, he folded it into a triangle, then loosely knotted it around his neck, cowboy style. *Too bad there's no mirror,* Tad thought. *I probably look just like Tad Miller, Rider of the Range.* He laughed at the thought.

He lay down again, glad he was no longer afraid. As he tried to get comfortable, he felt a sudden, strange pressure around his throat.

Thinking he had tied the bandanna too tight, Tad reached up to loosen the knot. It wouldn't come undone. The knot was small and tight, much tighter than he remembered tying it. It resisted his fingers as he tried to pick it apart.

Tad sat up again, taking a good grip on the bandanna and pulling. The more he tried to loosen the knot, the tighter it got. The bandanna was beginning to dig uncomfortably into his neck.

Tad tried to yank the whole thing up and over his head. *I'll be able to untie the knot when I can see it in front of my face,* he thought.

The cloth slipped from his fingers. It felt as if unseen hands were tugging on it, tightening the bandanna from behind him.

The cotton cloth started cutting into his throat like a noose. Tad's heart began to pound wildly as he struggled for air. He was choking, and in sudden panic he realized that his breathing was now completely cut off.

Tad tried to call out for help. The tiniest sound came from his throat. No one seemed to hear.

Frantically Tad clutched at his throat, trying to get his fingers under the cloth to pull it loose. His lungs were burning because he couldn't suck in any air.

His fingers couldn't get a grip on the bandanna. It was too tight, and growing tighter. It was cutting deep into his flesh now.

Blood pounded in Tad's head. Dark spots appeared before his eyes. He clawed at the bandanna. Even as he tried, his fingers grew weaker. The world was spinning around him.

How? he wondered. *How could a simple piece of cloth be strangling me?*

Chapter 3

TAD heard a roaring in his ears as the bandanna dug even tighter into his neck. The cloth gave a hard jerk, as if someone were trying to pull him backward, out of his sleeping bag.

Tad resisted fiercely. He was sure that if he gave in to that pull, he'd never breathe again.

He twisted around in his sleeping bag, hoping to catch his attacker. No one was behind him. He struggled to his knees, trying to fight the invisible pulling.

Then a hand yanked at his arm. "Tad?" said Sam's voice. "Are you all right?"

Tad's eyes were full of terror as he struggled with the bandanna. He had no breath left to tell Sam, to warn her, to beg for help.

"What in the world are you doing?" Sam sounded annoyed. "Don't you know how to tie a knot?" As soon as her hands went to untie the ends, the bandanna loosened. Tad gasped for air.

"Tad?" Sam's annoyance changed to concern. "What's going on?"

"I almost choked," Tad rasped, rubbing his sore neck. "It felt like—like someone was using the bandanna to strangle me. They were trying to drag me off this hill."

Sam stood up and looked around. Everyone was sleeping around the dying campfire. "There's no one up but us," she whispered. "All the other kids are asleep." She looked at him closely. "Are you sure you're okay?"

"I'm fine—now," said Tad. He frowned at the bandanna that had almost choked him. Now it was just a limp rag. Seconds earlier it had come close to killing him.

Sam stared at the bandanna too. "Didn't you find that when the gho—" She suddenly stopped. "When we were out getting wood?"

He nodded, his glance moving from the cloth to the campfire. "Yes," Tad said. "I should never have picked it up." He threw the bandanna into the fire. The two friends silently watched as it burned to ashes.

"I hope when I wake up, this will just turn out to be a weird dream," Sam said, shivering.

"That makes two of us," Tad said.

They both crawled back into their sleeping bags.

★   ★   ★

After breakfast the next morning, Mr. Taylor led the Chilleen students up and across the ridge and down into Kittredge.

Tad let his horse walk at its own pace as he checked out the ghost town. In the bright sunlight, he saw that the wooden buildings were old and weather-beaten. If there were any ghosts around, they seemed to have taken the morning off.

On the main street, he saw a run-down building with a dangling sign that read *Barber*. Next to it was a store that was called *Dry-Goods Emporium*. Faded lettering identified another building as the *Last Chance Saloon*. Except for the old livery stable at the edge of town, the buildings were only one story.

"I think this is awesome!" cried Monica Case, who'd gotten down from her horse. She stood in front of the old jailhouse. "It's just like in the movies!" She pointed her two index fingers as if they were guns. "I've got you covered!" she cried.

"You're dead!" exclaimed Randy, pretending to shoot back with his finger.

"Aargh! Got me!" cried Monica. She did a backflip over the hitching post and landed on the board sidewalk.

Everyone started laughing, including Mr. Taylor, but then he walked over to the rickety sidewalk. "I want you kids to be careful around here," he said. "The buildings are old and probably ready to fall down," he warned. "There could be spiders and snakes just about anywhere. So walk easy, and look before you poke into anything. I've never had an accident on any of my field trips. And," he said, "I don't want to ruin my record now."

As the teacher finished talking, a short man stepped out of the jailhouse doorway. He wore jeans and a collarless shirt. A floppy cowboy hat covered his eyes and shaded his smiling, bearded face. "Welcome to Kittredge!" the stranger said.

For an instant Tad thought he was seeing another ghost. Then Mr. Taylor said, "Kids, meet Pete Stone."

"I'm the mayor of Kittredge," Stone said, grinning. "I'm also the sheriff, stable owner—and the only person who lives here. Sometimes I pan the river for gold. In my off time, I greet visitors."

Tad thought the man must have a lot of free time. From what he'd read, the last gold miners had left Kittredge over a hundred years ago.

Pete Stone pointed to the jailhouse. "Some of the bravest marshals in the West worked here. And some of the biggest outlaws ended up behind those bars."

"Is this where Red Clarkson and Johnny Bodine shot it out?" Jeff asked.

Stone shook his head. "Nope. That happened outside the Last Chance. Red spent a lot of his time over there. There's a great story about a cowpoke who sat down with some friends and started talking about shooting the Last Chance up. As he drew his gun, he was pulled out of his chair by his ear, like a naughty schoolboy. His friends just sat where they were, staring at the floor.

The cowpoke was furious—until he saw who had him. 'Red Clarkson!' he said. 'I didn't know you had a piece of this place!' Everyone respected Red—and feared him. Red told him to make trouble in the next town. It was only a three-day ride away."

"You mean to say the local marshal owned the saloon?" Monica asked in disbelief.

"He was a partner in it," said Stone. "And he made sure there was no trouble there." The bearded man chuckled. "Lots of sheriffs and marshals had deals like that. Wyatt Earp owned part of a bar in Tombstone. Judge Roy Bean owned his own place too," explained Stone.

"That's something you don't usually think of when you hear about western heroes," Monica said doubtfully.

"This here town's full of stuff you don't read about in history books," said Stone. "Come on, I'll give you a tour."

Sam leaned over to Tad. "Let's take a peek in the saloon," she whispered. He nodded.

As Pete Stone led the way toward Kittredge's town hall, Tad and Sam fell back to the rear of the group. When the students reached the Last Chance, the two slipped through the saloon's half doors, which swung open and stayed that way.

Tad blinked as his eyes adjusted to the darkness. The few pieces of furniture were covered in dust. A beat-up piano stood in the corner. Several portraits hung on the wall opposite a long oak bar. A huge mirror lined the wall behind the bar. "Well, at least I don't see any ghosts," Tad said.

"Very funny," Sam said, walking over to the bar. She hoisted herself up on the dusty bar top and hopped down behind it.

"Hey," Tad said. "I thought we were just going to take a quick look, not go poking around."

Sam winked at him in the mirror and then ducked down behind the bar.

Curious, Tad climbed behind the bar. There were several empty shelves and boxes. Everything was covered with cobwebs. Remembering Mr. Taylor's warning about spiders, Tad began to carefully poke inside the boxes. Sam began feeling through the shelves with him.

"Tad, check it out!" cried Sam, pulling out a small, rusty rock pick and chisel.

Tad examined the old tools carefully. "I think these are miners' tools," he said. "These shelves were probably used for people to keep their things on while they were in the bar."

"I wish I could have lived here then," said Sam. "It must have been so exciting. In fact, I wish—" All of a sudden the room, which had been stuffy and warm, grew cold. Everything became dark, as if a cloud had passed in front of the sun.

The two friends stared out at the swinging doors. They could just make out two men standing outside in the bright sunshine. One man appeared to be tall and lanky with no hat. His hair and mustache were bright red. The other man was small, but when he moved, it was with the grace of a killer cat. Both men had grasped an end of a yellow bandanna with their left hands. Each man's right hand hovered at his gun belt.

"What are they doing?" Sam's voice was hoarse.

"It's a handkerchief duel," Tad said. "I've read about it. Each man holds on to the opposite end of a hankerchief with one hand. With their other hand they pull their guns and shoot."

"But they're right on top of each other!" Sam protested. "They'll both be killed."

Even as she spoke, the men whipped out their guns. They moved so quickly, their hands were just blurs.

The small man was young and fast. His gun was up and out a fraction of an instant before the redheaded man's weapon. It looked as if the redhead would surely die.

Then Tad saw another figure, a dim figure crouched just inside the room. The man had a pistol, and it was aimed at the short gunfighter outside. The figure's gun muzzle flashed, just as the small man's gun fired.

Both of the gunfighters jerked back. The small man clutched his shoulder. The tall man grabbed his leg. They both seemed to fall to the ground in slow motion.

"That redheaded guy cheated!" Sam burst out. "He had someone waiting to shoot the little man."

Tad gasped. He saw the figure inside fade into nothingness. He couldn't believe he just witnessed a shootout between ghosts!

Tad and Sam jumped out from behind the bar and ran outside. The two gunfighters lay on the ground. On top of the short man's chest was a piece of cloth. Tad's blood froze. It looked like the same yellow bandanna he'd found on his boot up on the ridge!

Before Tad's eyes, the two men and the cloth began to fade until they were only mist. The mist floated off down the street, past the train station at the edge of town.

Then Tad felt a fluttering at his chest. He glanced down. There, its edge peeking out from the top of his pocket, was the yellow bandanna.

Chapter 4

TAD slowly pulled the bandanna from his pocket. It looked exactly like the one he had found the day before—the one that had nearly strangled him.

For a moment he could almost feel the pressure around his throat, that choking feeling again. Tad quickly pushed the memory away.

"Where did *that* come from?" Sam cried. She shrank away from him, her green eyes round and big.

"I don't know where it came from, or how it got here," Tad whispered miserably.

"But it looks like the one you burned in the fire yesterday!" Sam exclaimed.

"I don't think it's exactly the same," said Tad, examining it closely. The pattern didn't seem quite the same, although he wasn't sure what the differences were.

Tad crumpled the square of cloth in his hands. This

couldn't possibly be the same bandanna he'd burned up. Still, how had it gotten in his pocket?

It gave him the creeps just to hold it. He decided to throw it away, but stopped. He didn't know what was going on, but a gut feeling told him the bandanna could be important.

"We've got to get to the bottom of this," Sam said. "That mist from the ghosts headed out of the town. Let's follow it."

"Follow ghosts?" Tad repeated. He didn't think it was a good idea at all.

"Please, Tad," Sam pleaded. "I *have* to. If you won't come, I'll go alone."

Tad wasn't about to let her go by herself. "Okay, I'll go," he muttered. "But what about Mr. Taylor and the others?"

Sam glanced down the street in both directions. The street was empty. "Mr. Taylor and the rest of the kids must still be inside one of the buildings."

"I don't know how I let you talk me into these things," Tad said. Learning about the Old West this way was something he wasn't sure he liked.

"Come *on*," she said. "Don't you want to find out what's going on?" Without waiting for an answer, she took off down the street.

Tad caught up with Sam at the end of the road. Beyond the town to the north was scrub brush leading to a high bluff. "Where do we go now?" he asked.

"The mist must have been blown up the bluff," Sam

guessed. They carefully picked their way through the brush and then up the loose gravel and rocks to the top of the bluff. "Wow," Tad said. The slope was very steep down into the canyon on the other side. "It's a long way down into that canyon."

"There must have been a trail up here when Kittredge was still a town," said Sam. "Maybe we can find what's left of it."

"Okay," Tad agreed. They walked along the narrow rim looking for any trails that led down to the canyon floor. Tad saw that there was no way to gain a foothold on the bare rock face.

"Over here!" cried Sam suddenly. Tad turned to where she was pointing. There was a very narrow trail zigzagging down the cliff to a small hill that rose out of the canyon floor.

With Sam leading the way, they started down the trail to the hill. It was very steep and covered with tiny rocks. Several times Tad almost slipped. He realized that cowboy boots weren't much good on loose rock.

Then the trail ended suddenly. A pile of fallen rock and dirt had covered it over. Tad brushed some sweat off his forehead. By now the sun was high overhead.

"Let's give it up," he said to Sam. He wasn't about to risk climbing over the rock. "I don't think anyone's used this trail in a hundred years."

"Nobody who's alive, at least," said Sam, sighing. "We might as well go back. Mr. Taylor's probably sent the sheriff after us by now." They both laughed at the thought.

They turned back and began retracing their steps up to the top of the canyon wall.

"Well, I guess my brilliant idea of chasing ghosts was a complete bust. . . ." Sam's voice trailed off. She stared upward. "What's that?" she whispered.

Tad raised his eyes too. At the top of the canyon wall, a large cottonwood tree spread its branches. Tad was sure it hadn't been there before. It was hard to see clearly, but there seemed to be a crowd gathered around it.

"Who are they?" he asked. "What are they doing there?"

"Maybe they're tourists," Sam said, her voice full of doubt.

Tad squinted against the sun to get a closer look at the crowd. The people seemed to be covered by shadows, even though it was a clear day. "They're all grown-ups," he finally said. "But how could a tour group come by?"

"Hey," Sam exclaimed, "all those people are dressed in old-fashioned clothes!"

Suddenly the view snapped into focus, and Tad could make the people out more clearly. He saw that Sam was right. All the people were dressed in cowboy clothes or old-fashioned suits. The few women in the crowd wore long dresses. One woman even carried a parasol.

"What are they doing?" Sam asked.

Tad felt a cold prickle at the back of his neck. "Sam," he gulped, "I think they're all *ghosts*."

They inched up the trail and hid behind a rock about ten feet below the rim. From their hiding spot they could clearly see the people in the crowd and the tree. To one side of the tree a small wooden platform had been built.

Everyone in the crowd was staring at the platform. It looked as if they were waiting for something to happen. Tad began picking his way up the trail again. Just then a tall, red-haired man stepped up to the canyon's edge and began scanning the landscape below. He was looking right at Tad! No, he was looking right *through* Tad, as if he didn't see him at all.

"I—I think you're right," Sam said, her voice sounding spooked. "Those people *are* all ghosts." She crept up to Tad's side.

"That's probably the whole town of Kittredge," said Tad. The two stared up at the crowd on the edge of the cliff.

The tall, redheaded man stepped onto the platform. He was dressed in a black three-piece suit, his hair was carefully combed, and his red mustache had been waxed into points. He walked stiffly, supporting himself with a cane. Something glinted on his vest. It was a star!

"Sam!" Tad whispered to his friend. "I just realized who that man has to be. The red hair, the badge—it's Marshal Red Clarkson!"

Clarkson pulled something out of his pocket and waved it to the crowd. Tad recognized that too. It was the yellow bandanna. The crowd raised their fists. It looked as if they were shouting, but neither Sam nor Tad could hear anything.

"If that's Red Clarkson," Sam said slowly, "then the other man in the gunfight had to be—look over there!"

Tad looked past the crowd and saw a group of men walking along the rim toward the tree. Two of them were pushing along a third man, who was staring down at the ground. His wrists were handcuffed together. Then he lifted his head. Tad shivered as he recognized the man's face.

It was the other gunman from the handkerchief duel. Tad knew this had to be Johnny Bodine.

Bodine glanced over the crowd, then looked down into the canyon. Tad and Sam didn't try to hide, since they were sure he couldn't see them. The outlaw's dark gaze settled on Tad. The hair on Tad's neck rose as Johnny gave him a faint smile. He and his guards continued to walk, slowly, toward the tree.

The crowd parted as they got near the platform. Red Clarkson stood waiting at the top of the short set of steps. Bodine stood up even straighter when he saw his enemy.

Now the marshal reached up onto a tree branch and pulled down a long rope. "Wait a minute," Sam said, her voice high. "What are they doing?"

Tad didn't say a word. The rope had a special kind of knot. The end was coiled thirteen times around the rope before it ended in a large loop. It was a hangman's knot. There had to be thirteen coils in the hangman's knot, Tad remembered reading. Otherwise the prisoner's neck wouldn't break.

While Bodine stood there, calm and unmoving, Red Clarkson showed the rope to the crowd.

Then the marshal took the loop and placed it around the young outlaw's neck. Still Johnny Bodine showed no emotion.

Samantha Vance did.

"No!" she screamed. "You can't get away with it! First you cheated at the shoot-out. And now you're going to hang Johnny Bodine!"

Chapter 5

TAD grabbed Sam's arm as she started climbing the short distance to the canyon rim. "You can't change anything," he told her. "This is what happened in history. We're seeing something that took place a long time ago. But I think Johnny Bodine does know we're here," continued Tad. "He looked right at me and smiled."

Sam's eyes widened in surprise. "H-he did?" She gasped and looked up.

Above them, Red Clarkson tightened the noose around Bodine's neck. He stood to one side of the platform, facing the crowd, and made a speech. Tad and Sam could see the lawman's lips moving, but they couldn't hear what he said. It was eerie, watching the scene silently unfold.

At last Clarkson turned back to Bodine. This time

Tad could read the marshal's lips: "Do you have any last words?"

For a long moment Bodine just stared into Red Clarkson's eyes. Then, with a bitter smile, he shook his head.

The marshal stepped back and raised his hand to signal the hangman. Suddenly Bodine brought up his cuffed hands and grabbed Clarkson. Tad thought the outlaw was trying to strangle the lawman. Instead, he grabbed something that had been hanging around Clarkson's neck.

"This is not the last of me!" Bodine cried to the crowd. Then he threw whatever he'd grabbed down into the canyon.

To Tad's surprise, the twinkling object came flying down right at him. It fell into his hands.

"What's that?" cried Sam.

Tad opened his hands. Lying on his palm was an old-fashioned metal key on a torn leather thong. Carved into the long shank of the key were the letters: *AHTAWAIH*.

"Ahtawaih?" Tad said, baffled.

As the word left his lips, the sky suddenly darkened. A huge black cloud cut off the sun. The world became bitterly cold, and Tad and Sam clung together. A wild wind wailed around them.

A moment later, the sun returned. Tad looked up. But there was no cottonwood tree, no townspeople, and no Johnny Bodine on the canyon rim.

He turned to Sam, shaking. "What's going on? First the bandanna, now the key. And we *heard* the ghost speak! This is beyond scary!"

Sam looked sadly at him. "I think it may be all my fault," she said.

"How can it be your fault?" Tad wanted to know.

"Johnny Bodine had a sister. She married a man named Ike Vance, and they set up a ranch near here. I'm their great-great-granddaughter."

Tad stared. "You mean, you're related to Johnny Bodine? I mean, I know your family lived near here— I just hadn't guessed how long."

"Maybe we heard him because I'm his relative," Sam said.

Tad smiled. "I guess that's why you wanted to come on the Kittredge trip so much."

"My parents weren't that interested in history, so we never came here," said Sam. "I had to see it in person. And . . . I wanted a chance to find out the truth about Johnny Bodine."

Tad shook his head. "Well, we're certainly finding out some weird stuff."

She looked at him. "Maybe you think it's silly of me to worry about a relative from so long ago."

Tad only shrugged. "Hey, at least you've got a cool one. I only wish I had a great-great-granduncle like Johnny Bodine. He sure beats Thaddeus Miller."

"Who's he?" Sam asked.

"Oh, that's my great-great-great-grandfather. He

headed for California in 1849—the big gold rush. When
he couldn't hack it as a prospector, he settled in San
Francisco. Then he made a fortune running a laundry
service."

Sam stared. "A laundry?"

"Everyone was so busy looking for gold, nobody had
time for anything else. People had to send their dirty
laundry off on boats to be washed in Hawaii. Then
Thaddeus came along and cleaned up—in more ways
than one." Tad laughed. "My family has lived in the
city ever since. In a way, it's because of him that I read
so much about the Old West. I always wanted to see
what it was really like to be a pioneer."

Sam smiled. "I guess you're seeing more than you
ever thought you would."

"So are you," said Tad. "You've seen Johnny
Bodine's last gunfight, and you just saw him about to
be hanged." He looked down at the key in his hand
and wrapped it in the bandanna. "Now we've got
this."

"Johnny wanted us to have that key," Sam said.
"That means there's something in Kittredge to be
unlocked."

Tad nodded. "All we have to do is find it."

They started up the old trail. When they reached
the top they saw Pete Stone walking toward them. The
unofficial mayor of Kittredge looked worried. "Your
teacher sent me off to search for you," he said.

"We saw the most incredible thing!" Sam said. Tad

felt a little uncomfortable as she told about the shoot-out and the hanging. Did Sam have to tell everybody about this weird stuff? So far, everyone thought they were making up wild stories.

"And we wound up with this key!" Sam finished, getting Tad to take the key out.

"I guess you see strange stuff like this all the time, living here." Tad wrapped the key back in the bandanna and shoved it in his back pocket.

Pete Stone looked very serious. "You can bet I hear a lot of stories like this," he said. "But maybe you shouldn't talk about it. The other kids might get scared, or they won't believe you."

"Sounds like a good idea," said Tad. He wasn't in the mood to hear stupid jokes about ghost stories again.

For the rest of the day they quietly listened as Mr. Taylor discussed the town's history. Several times he mentioned Johnny Bodine and Red Clarkson.

"Bodine and Clarkson started out as good friends," the teacher said. "They rode together as cowboys. Then Clarkson became a marshal. Bodine began breaking the law, often to help out people who had money trouble. That made Johnny Bodine lots of friends in the valley. But it didn't make Clarkson too happy."

Mr. Taylor went on. "There's a story that Johnny gave the owner of the Kittredge general store a thousand dollars right after his store burned down. All the man had left was a small pile of goods."

"Why did he do that?" Randy asked.

"Because that store owner had let Bodine's father buy food on credit when Johnny was a little boy, and now he was paying back the favor," Mr. Taylor said. The teacher shook his head. "Finally, however, Bodine robbed the Cannonball, killing Zeb Frobisher, the clerk in the mail car."

"Did anybody ever find the money he stole?" Jane wondered.

"No," Randy told her. "People think Johnny Bodine's treasure is still hidden somewhere in Kittredge."

"Bodine said he never stole that money," Sam spoke up. "And said he didn't kill Zeb Frobisher."

"It was the only killing Bodine was ever accused of," Mr. Taylor said. "But it was enough to get him hanged. Although the robber hid his face, Red Clarkson had a couple witnesses on the train who were able to identify Bodine. They recognized the yellow bandanna he wore as a mask. It was Johnny Bodine's trademark. The town turned against Johnny, and he was found guilty of murder."

Sam and Tad looked at each other. That helped to make sense of several things they had seen. Or did it? Once again, Tad examined the bandanna that had mysteriously appeared in his pocket after the duel.

After Mr. Taylor's lecture, they set up camp in the ghost town. Pete Stone reopened the livery stable for their horses. They built a fire outside the building and dumped their gear around it.

It was just about sundown now, and the kids were sitting around the campfire. Randy, Jeff, and Monica were in charge of dinner, and it was almost ready.

"Some days I wish I were a horse," Randy said, laughing. "No cooking for me. I'd just sit down with a nice bale of hay."

"If you're that hungry," Jeff joked, "you can go in and see if the horses will share with you." He pointed through the open doors of the livery stable.

Just then Tad heard a noise. It sounded like angry whining. "What's—"

"It's the horses!" Sam cut him off. "Something's wrong with the horses!"

Now Tad recognized the sound of whinnying. He and the others ran into the building. They had stabled the horses in the back of the long, narrow building. Inside, the horses were rearing and pawing the air in their stalls. Their eyes were wild with fear. A chill filled the stable.

"There's nothing here," Randy cried, puzzled.

"I wonder what's spooking them," Monica said. She and the others began inching toward the horses to try to calm them.

Tad stood frozen in the doorway, though. There, in the middle of the stable, was the ghost of Red Clarkson, a look of hatred on his face.

"Walk slowly," Mr. Taylor directed, "or we'll spook them more."

Tad couldn't believe his friends. Couldn't they see Clarkson waving his arms to excite the horses?

Completely wild now, the horses tore loose almost all at once. With terrified neighs and a pounding of hooves, they broke down the dry and rotted wood of their stalls and charged for the livery door—straight toward the students!

Chapter 6

"STAMPEDE!"

The cry echoed over the pounding hoofbeats and frightened whinnies of the horses.

Tad could hear the terrified screams of the other kids as they passed him. He was still standing just inside the door.

"Move!" someone shrieked. "Come on! *Move!*"

Monica twisted her ankle and fell. "Help!" she screamed as the kids raced past her. In seconds the horses would be on top of her.

Already the big animals were too close. Foam dripped from their mouths, and the sound of their hoofbeats was like thunder.

Without thinking, Tad leaped the fifteen feet and lunged for Monica. He pulled her out of the horses' path seconds before the animals were on them.

The lead horse, a white stallion that belonged to Mr. Taylor, was almost halfway out the door when it suddenly calmed and stopped. The other horses pulled up too, snorting quietly and pawing at the ground.

Tad looked up from the dirt floor and saw the ghost of Red Clarkson laughing soundlessly as he faded into nothing.

The horses had sensed the ghost's presence and quieted down as soon as he was no longer a threat.

Tad let out the breath he'd been holding. The terrible cold was gone with Red Clarkson.

Mr. Taylor and the other kids came back inside. They crowded around Monica and Tad. Monica tested her ankle, and it was okay.

"What happened?" cried Monica. "Why did they act so crazy all of a sudden?"

"I—I don't know!" said Randy, his voice shaking.

"Everything's going to be all right," Mr. Taylor said, but even he sounded frightened. "We should be glad that we're all okay," he continued. "And that the horses didn't get hurt."

Mr. Taylor directed the students to tie the horses in their stalls. Soon everyone else was back at the campfire.

"Lucky for you guys that we're great cooks," Randy said. "Nothing even burned."

Everyone laughed at Randy's joke, and Tad felt some of the tension ease.

As the kids finished fixing dinner, Sam approached

their teacher. "I have to tell you something, Mr. Taylor."

Tad felt a chill run down his spine. *Had Sam seen Red Clarkson too?* She had. He watched as Sam grabbed the teacher's arm, taking him aside. "You may not believe this," she said, "but those horses were spooked by a ghost."

"I saw it," Tad said, joining them. "And I know who it was—Red Clarkson!"

Mr. Taylor frowned as if he were trying to understand what they were telling him. "Red Clarkson?" he repeated.

Between the two of them, Tad and Sam told the story of what had happened to them that day. Mr. Taylor seemed more nervous than angry.

"I've heard it said that animals can see things people sometimes can't," the teacher admitted. "But I still want to check that it wasn't a live human intruder who set the horses off."

He glanced at the other students. "We won't talk about this in front of them, but I'll check with Pete Stone and make a little search later."

Everyone was very quiet during dinner, and no one suggested telling ghost stories. While Monica and Jeff cleaned up after dinner, the rest of the kids got ready for bed.

Tad unrolled his sleeping bag and air mattress. Sam was already in her bedroll, her eyes half-shut as she gazed up at the sparkling stars.

After everyone had been lying down for a while, Tad saw Mr. Taylor quietly pick up his pack and start toward the middle of town. Tad waited until Mr. Taylor was gone before he sat up by the fire. The mysterious word on the key kept coming to his mind. He knew he wouldn't be able to sleep until he tried to figure out what it meant.

Setting a notebook across his lap, Tad pulled out a pencil and the key that Johnny Bodine had thrown at him. He started scribbling away.

"Tad?" It was Sam, whispering to him.

"Uh-huh?"

"You couldn't sleep?"

Tad shook his head. "How could I?" he said.

"It's safe now," said Sam. "The horses won't get loose again. We made sure they're all tied securely."

"Unless Red Clarkson spooks them again." Tad shook his head. "You saw him and I saw him, but nobody else saw Clarkson spooking our horses."

"Spooking is right." Sam sat up now, wrapping her arms around herself as if she were cold. "What are you doing?" she asked.

"I'm trying to make sense out of those letters on the key," Tad whispered. "Maybe they're jumbled words." He frowned as he kept writing with his pencil.

"Did you get anything?" Sam finally asked.

"I can make words out of the letters, but they don't make any sense. Here's one. *A HAT I HAW.* That uses all the letters, but doesn't tell us much."

Sam chuckled softly. "I can see what you mean."

"How about this one? *WHAT I AHA.*" Tad shook his head. "Then there's my favorite. *WAIT HA HA.* Maybe Johnny Bodine was just having some fun with us."

"No," Sam said. "That key fits a lock somewhere. I'll bet it turns out to be a strongbox."

"A strongbox?"

"In the old days people hid their valuables in heavy boxes with locks on them," Sam told him. "We've still got our old family strongbox. It used to be buried behind our ranch house."

Tad blinked in confusion. "There was a bank here in Kittredge. Why didn't people keep their valuables there?"

"Banks weren't always safe. A bank could go broke. Or it could be robbed by outlaws."

"Like Johnny Bodine?" Tad asked with a smile.

"There were lots of other outlaws around," Sam said. "Lots worse than Johnny Bodine."

Tad looked back down at his paper and yawned. He was getting nowhere.

"Maybe it's a code," Sam suggested. She sounded tired too.

"I'll sleep on it," said Tad. Putting his stuff away, he lay back down. Moments later they both drifted off to sleep.

They woke in the morning to sounds of an uproar. "Mr. Taylor!" Jeff was calling. "Mr. Taylor! Where are you?"

Tad blinked his eyes and pulled himself into a sitting position. "What's going on?" he asked in a fuzzy voice, still half-asleep.

"Yeah," Sam said, "what's happening?"

Tad found himself staring into Randy Moser's scared brown eyes.

"It's Mr. Taylor," Randy said. "He's gone!"

Chapter 7

RANDY'S words jolted Tad fully awake.

"Mr. Taylor's gone?" asked Tad, not sure he had heard correctly.

"Yes, and he's been gone for a long time!" Jane Trent exclaimed, nervously twirling one of her red curls.

Monica pointed to the space where their teacher had set up for the night. "Look!" she said. "His sleeping bag hasn't even been slept in!"

"What could have happened to him?" Jeff asked in a frightened whisper.

"And what are we supposed to do?" Jane sounded scared.

Sam and Tad felt guilty. Mr. Taylor had told them he intended to check out their story last night. Both of them had seen him go off. Now he hadn't come back!

"I think the first thing we should do is find Pete Stone," Sam said, trying to stay calm. "He knows the town and can help us look for Mr. Taylor."

"I'll go," Randy offered. He dashed off to get the only other adult who was in Kittredge.

Soon he came rushing back—alone. "Pete Stone isn't around either," Randy reported, out of breath. "I checked all around the house he uses, and I couldn't find him."

"M-maybe ghosts got them," Jane said, her voice trembling. "Maybe they got Mr. Taylor and Mr. Stone."

"Mr. Taylor had a reason for going out last night," Tad said. "After our horses got spooked, he said he was going to take a look around." He glanced down at the teacher's untouched sleeping bag. "It looks like he never came back."

"This isn't the greatest place in the world to go wandering around at night," Sam said.

"What about Pete Stone?" Randy challenged. "Why is he gone too?"

Tad shrugged. "Maybe he decided to go prospecting. We can't tell. Our problem right now is Mr. Taylor." He looked at Randy. "Does Pete Stone have a phone in his house?"

Randy shook his head. "I looked. There's no phone, no radio, no way to call for help." He paused. "Unless one of us rides to get some."

"Lee, the school handyman, is driving out to meet

us the day after tomorrow to help us take some of our stuff back to Chilleen," Sam pointed out. "None of us knows the area well enough to make it back to school all alone."

"Why don't we put it to a vote?" Tad suggested. "Those in favor of riding into the desert to find help, raise their hands."

Randy and Jeff put up their hands.

"Against?"

Tad, Sam, Monica, and Jane all raised their hands.

Randy shook his head in disgust. "Trust the city boy to vote to stay put."

"That's because I think staying put is the safest plan. Who knows how long it could take to find help, and none of us even knows which way to go," Tad said.

"Okay," Randy said sulkily. "So what do we do?"

Tad spoke first. "We'll break into search parties and check out the area. Pick a partner. Nobody should go off alone."

He and Sam chose to work together. They agreed to check out the barber shop and the Last Chance Saloon in the middle of the main street. Monica and Randy were searching the livery stable and the buildings on that side of town. Jeff and Jane went to look in the old boardinghouse and the surrounding area.

The old barber shop was a tiny building off the wooden sidewalk. In front stood a long wooden pole, once painted with red, white, and blue strips. Years of strong sun had faded the colors to pale pink, gray, and grayer.

A cloud of dust kicked up when Sam and Tad opened the door to the old building. The old shop was very tiny, more like a closet than a room. A cracked mirror ran along one wall.

In the center of the floor stood two barber chairs. "Nothing in here," Sam said. "The dust's so thick on the floor that if Mr. Taylor had been here, we would have seen his footprints."

"Let's check the saloon," Tad said. The two walked over to the bar, but no one was inside. Sam was very quiet as they poked around in the huge old bar.

"Maybe Mr. Taylor went upstairs and got hurt somehow," Tad said, thinking aloud. He gazed up at the balcony that overlooked the room. "Mr. Taylor!" he called.

From the distance, he heard the other kids' voices shouting the teacher's name.

"I feel awful about this," Sam confessed. "That trouble last night was because of us—because Red Clarkson's ghost was after us. Mr. Taylor went off to check, and now he's gone." She shook her head. "I just feel it's all our fault."

Together they climbed the rickety stairs to the second floor. No one was in the upper rooms.

What if Mr. Taylor was stranded somewhere? What if he was hurt? Maybe he couldn't even hear them calling him. "Does this place have a basement?" Tad asked as they returned downstairs.

"I don't think these western buildings had basements." Sam went off to check what used to be the kitchen, while Tad paced the barroom. He carefully checked the floorboards as he walked. Maybe Mr. Taylor had crashed through a floor. Tad didn't want that to happen to him. He walked along the wall with all the paintings. The first picture hung from the wall in a gold-colored frame. Though now dusty and faded, the picture clearly showed a beautiful young blond woman in a red dress. A smaller picture hung next to it. This one was a faded color print, under glass. It showed a not very realistic picture of a Native American warrior. Fancy letters showed his name, Hiawatha.

Tad passed a third picture—and froze. The portrait was crude, but he still recognized the subject's grinning face.

It was Johnny Bodine. A little plaque on the frame gave the date of the outlaw's hanging. Tad was more interested in one of the small details of the painting, though. Bodine wore a dark hat and shirt. Around his neck was a bandanna. It was yellow—and it looked just like the one Tad now carried!

"Tad, why aren't you—look out!" Sam's terrified scream broke into his thoughts. A moment later a glass shattered noiselessly against the wall inches from his head.

"Watch out!" Sam screamed again. She dashed over, grabbed Tad's shirt, and pulled him to the floor. Another glass flew past the spot Tad's head had been just a moment before. His heart thudding, Tad glanced back at the bar and froze.

Standing behind the old oak bar was the man he and Sam knew as Red Clarkson. The marshal's face was set in a snarl of hatred. He had his hand on a rack of glasses that hadn't been there before. Tad watched, terrified and helpless, as the man grabbed another glass and hurled it at them.

Tad wasn't sure if the ghost's glasses could really hurt them, but he didn't want to find out the hard way. Quickly Tad rolled over, pulling Sam with him. Another glass smashed soundlessly into the wall, and then another. Faster and faster they came. Every time Tad and Sam made a move, Clarkson aimed another glass. Faster and faster, closer and closer, the glasses came.

"Stop! Stop! Please stop!" Sam was crying now, pleading with the ghost. But he acted as if he didn't hear her. Tad could now see that the rack of glasses was nearly gone. In another moment Red Clarkson would have thrown all the glasses left in the bar. Then he and Sam could escape.

Two more shattered just above their heads.

There were no more glasses!

"Come on, Sam!" Tad shouted, pulling his friend up. They started for the door.

Red Clarkson was moving too. Tad saw the angry marshal pick up an empty liquor bottle and smash it on the edge of the bar. Holding the sharp, jagged glass in his hands, he leapt over the bar, blocking the way out.

There was no way they could get past Clarkson. The

ghost began to walk toward them. He moved slowly, limping with his stiff leg, waving the broken bottle in his hand. Then he raised his empty hand and pulled it across his neck.

Tad understood the grim meaning behind the ghost's gesture. Marshal Red Clarkson was going to cut their throats!

Chapter 8

"**N**O!" Tad yelled. "Get away!" He pushed Sam behind him and began backing up.

Red Clarkson's lips moved, but Tad and Sam couldn't hear what he was saying. All Tad knew was that the marshal continued to come toward them, dragging his stiff leg. He held the jagged edges of the bottle out in front of him like a knife. A few more steps and Clarkson would be close enough to cut their throats.

"Stay next to me," Tad whispered to Sam as they inched backward. Tad's mouth was dry with fright. His eyes darted one way, then another. If only they could make a run for it!

He and Sam had nowhere to run, though. The ghost of Red Clarkson was blocking the only exit from the Last Chance Saloon.

Then Sam bumped into something hard. "We're against the wall," she whispered.

Now they were really cornered. Still moving slowly, as if to show he was in no hurry to kill them, Clarkson came closer and closer.

"Help!" Tad suddenly screamed. "Help!" If only the other Chilleen students could hear, maybe they'd be able to stop Clarkson.

"Help!" Sam joined in. She screamed at the top of her voice. "Somebody, help!"

Suddenly Tad saw a flicker of movement near the doors. From the corner of his eye, he saw Johnny Bodine appear. At first he was nothing more than a shadow. A moment later he was as solid as Clarkson. Bodine was dressed all in black, with the yellow bandanna around his neck. He had that same strange half smile on his face that Tad had seen before. Bodine stared straight at Tad, then drew his gun.

Tad felt his heart hammer even faster inside his chest. Beside him, Sam screamed again. He knew she was thinking the same thing he was. If Clarkson didn't kill them with the broken bottle, Bodine was going to shoot them!

"No!" Sam screamed. "No, no!"

He and Sam ducked just as they saw a flash from Bodine's gun. They raised their eyes as Bodine aimed again—not at them, but at Clarkson!

The lawman was staring at the hand where, a second before, he'd held the broken bottle. It was gone! Johnny

Bodine had shot it to nothingness! Quickly Clarkson drew his gun. In the same motion he fired back at Bodine. The bullet missed Bodine and bounced off the wall. Bodine fired back.

The air turned cold and began to fill with a thick haze of smoke. Sam's screams filled the air. Tad buried his head in his hands, trying to make himself as small as possible so he wouldn't be hit in the cross fire.

Then, suddenly, the temperature in the room rose.

Tad cautiously lifted his head. The air was clear and there was no sign of either Clarkson or Bodine or the shattered glasses. Standing in the doorway was Jeff Dearborn, staring at Tad and Sam.

"What's going on?" he asked. "From the noise you were making, I thought you'd found Mr. Taylor." Jeff was obviously worried. "Instead, I find the two of you all scrunched up against the wall and yelling."

"Y-you didn't see them?" Tad croaked. "Red Clarkson and Johnny Bodine. They were both here. Clarkson tried to kill us. He and Bodine shot at each other."

"You're kidding," Jeff said. He cast an uneasy glance around the room. "Okay. Tell me what happened."

Slowly, her voice trembling, Sam told the story of Clarkson's attack and the shoot-out. "We both saw the same thing," she finished. "Two people can't see the same thing if it's not real, can they, Jeff?"

Jeff didn't answer at first. Finally he said, "After all that's been happening, I *really* don't know."

★   ★   ★

"You're saying ghosts got Mr. Taylor?" Randy Moser's voice was heavy with disbelief. The students were back at the livery stable. None of them had found any trace of the teacher. Sam and Tad had told the others everything that had happened to them.

"Ghosts taking Mr. Taylor is like saying he disappeared into thin air," Jeff said. "I don't know what to say. I've heard stories about weird things happening in Kittredge. Maybe this is one of them."

"But saying that we're being haunted . . ." Randy shook his head.

"Maybe the rest of you don't believe in ghosts. But I think it's possible. And now we know that Sam is related to Johnny Bodine . . ." Monica's blue eyes looked troubled.

"So what are we going to do?" Jeff asked. "Just sit around and wait for Lee the day after tomorrow?"

"Well, I'm sure we'll be okay for that long," Tad said, "but I'm not so sure about Mr. Taylor. I'm going to keep looking for him. How about you guys?"

The Chilleen students looked scared, but they agreed. By late afternoon, however, there was still no sign of the teacher, and the kids were feeling pretty discouraged. They were all dirty and dusty from poking around town searching for their teacher.

Sam and Tad were tired. They'd pried up a trapdoor they'd found in the saloon's kitchen. All they'd found was a small storage space, and no trace of Mr. Taylor. Pete Stone hadn't returned from wherever he had gone.

Jane had been spooked by a big, ugly spider during her search. Now she was so scared that she refused to leave the camp again.

Everyone was very quiet as they ate the supper they had managed to work together to make. The meal didn't taste too good, but nobody said anything. They huddled together, staring into the campfire, and laid out their sleeping bags inside the livery stable. Nobody wanted to sleep outside.

"Let's get some rest," Tad told them. "We'll have to get up early tomorrow. We'll check out the canyon tomorrow. If we don't have any luck, we'll start riding into the desert."

By now the sun had gone down. No one mentioned the word *ghost*. Even so, thoughts of Johnny Bodine and Red Clarkson kept bothering Tad. He was glad there had been no more weird visits from them. As he drifted off to sleep, Tad hoped it would stay that way.

In his dream, he was all alone, walking down the main street of Kittredge. Everything was gray and misty. He headed toward the double doors of the Last Chance Saloon. As he pushed his way through the doors, Tad expected to see what the saloon was like in its glory days.

Instead, the Last Chance was just as dusty and run-down as it had been when he and Sam had explored it. Tad walked over to the wall with the pictures. He passed the picture of the woman in the red gown. Next came the warrior. Finally Tad came up to the portrait of Johnny Bodine—and stared.

This wasn't the crudely drawn painting he'd seen earlier. Bodine himself was peering out from the wooden frame, giving Tad that odd half smile. The outlaw's lips moved, but Tad didn't hear any words.

"I don't understand," he said, taking a step back.

Johnny Bodine leaned forward, coming out of the picture frame. He pointed back over Tad's shoulder, his lips still moving.

"I can't hear you," Tad said.

Bodine was obviously frustrated. He reached out to Tad and shoved his hand into Tad's shirt pocket. Bodine's hand clasped the metal key. Lips still moving silently, Bodine again pointed over Tad's shoulder at the bar.

Tad turned around. All he saw were the bar, the shelves, and the huge mirror on the wall. The images of Tad, Johnny Bodine, the warrior, and the lady in red were reflected in the mirror.

Their images faded as a huge pair of eyes glared at Tad from the mirror. They were narrow blue eyes, filled with evil. Tad recognized them immediately.

Red Clarkson!

Tad shuddered awake. *What a weird dream,* he thought, shivering. Taking a deep breath, he closed his eyes, trying to go back to sleep.

Tad's eyes opened again, and he sniffed. There was smoke in the air.

He sat up and peered into the darkness. A dull red glow was coming from a large bale of hay set aside for the horses.

Tad heard a crackling noise, and the glow grew brighter. Flames were dancing on the hay bale!

Tad's breath caught in his throat. Soon the livery stable where he and the others were sleeping would be ablaze.

Chapter 9

"WAKE up! Get up, everybody! There's a fire!" Tad tore out of his sleeping bag. He dashed among the five other Chilleen students, shaking them awake.

For a second there was total confusion. Then Jeff ran over to the bale of burning straw, carrying his sleeping bag. He slapped at the flames with the bag, trying to beat them down.

Tad saw in an instant that the fire had gotten too big for one boy to handle. It was about to spread to the other hay bales.

"I can't put it out!" Jeff shouted, still swatting with his bedding.

"We've got to get water if we're going to smother those flames!" cried Monica. "Let's try that old pump outside the building."

She and the others ran to the front doors. Just before

they reached them, the heavy old double doors slammed shut.

"Hey!" cried Monica. She pushed against one door. Tad and the others joined her.

"They're stuck!" yelled Randy. "These stupid things won't move at all!"

"How could they close in the first place?" Jane cried. Smoke was beginning to fill the stable, making it hard to breathe.

"Come on!" said Monica. "All together, one, two, three!" The students threw themselves against one door, but it remained immovable.

Tad could feel the heat building up behind them as the blaze grew. He heard the horses neighing and stomping in their stalls.

He looked back over his shoulder. The fire was slowly spreading. He could see its hot flames licking at the sides of one of the wooden horse stalls. In a moment, Tad realized, the horses would go wild. Then the trapped students would only have a choice between getting trampled or burning to death.

"Come *on*," Tad said. "We've got to keep trying!" He flung himself at the door, pushing with all his might. It gave a little, but the door was still jammed shut. Tad's heart was pounding like a jackhammer. He felt as if his lungs were on fire.

The other kids raced back to try to control the blaze again. Only Tad and Sam were left at the door.

Then Tad's eyes widened as he realized someone else had joined them. It wasn't one of the students, though.

It was Johnny Bodine! As usual, Bodine had his strange half smile on his face. He stared directly at Tad as if to say, *Don't give up.* Then Bodine placed his ghostly hands over Tad and Sam's. Tad could see his own hand *through* Bodine's. It was an eerie feeling.

Even more weird was how much stronger he felt. Tad pushed harder. Sam pushed with him. Johnny Bodine seemed to be laughing.

More strength flowed into the two kids. The door started to inch open. A moment later it flew open with a screech of old wood.

Tad whipped around, grabbed his sleeping bag, and ran to the pump. Sam and Johnny Bodine were there ahead of him. Together they pumped, and a stream of water poured out of the old pipe.

The water was red with rust, but Tad didn't care. He soaked the bag, then returned to the barn to fight the fire. The others saw what he was doing and quickly lent a hand, filling old buckets that had been in the stable and wetting their sleeping bags.

Working together, they were able to smother the flames. The horses whinnied and shied at the smoke, but quickly calmed down.

Tad surveyed the damage. The hay and straw were pretty much gone, and one of the horse stalls was scorched. Luckily, it had been empty. None of the camping supplies had been burnt. Except for the smoky smell, the livery stable seemed all right.

"Any idea what started the fire?" Randy asked. "I

don't suppose anyone lit a match in here. Did any of you try to get one of the old lamps going while the rest of us were asleep?"

The kids all shook their heads. Of the old kerosene lamps lying around the stable, only one still had a glass chimney. None were near where the fire had begun, Tad realized.

"Maybe a spark flew in from the campfire," Randy said, interrupting Tad's thoughts.

The campfire was almost out, though. It wouldn't be easy for a tiny flame to leap from those banked, glowing coals to ignite the straw yards away.

"I don't know what to say," Randy finally admitted.

Tad kept his worries to himself, not wanting to alarm the others. "Let's get down to business," he said. "We've still got lots of work to do around here."

The students hung up their wet sleeping bags to dry. Then they headed over to Pete Stone's house to raid his supplies. They managed to find extra blankets and a couple of spare bedrolls Stone must have kept for his prospecting expeditions. Pete Stone was still nowhere to be found.

"At least we have something to sleep in," Monica said.

Everyone decided to sleep outside, and Jeff and Randy built the fire up. By the time the kids had fixed up their camp, it was after midnight. Everyone but Sam and Tad soon fell into an exhausted sleep. The two friends sat up, wrapped in blankets, and talked for a while.

"I don't understand it," Tad said for about the eighth time. "Why is all this trouble aimed at us? We sure didn't do anything to make Red Clarkson mad at us. And you're a relative of Johnny Bodine's. Why would he want to hurt you?"

"He's helped us," Sam pointed out. "First he rescued us in the saloon, then he got the stable doors open."

"Yes, but that was after he nearly ran us over on his horse—and left me the amazing strangling bandanna." Tad shook his head and continued, "Red Clarkson, on the other hand, has always been after us. The stampede and that attack in the saloon. I'm sure he lit the fire. And I think that somehow he's growing in power."

"You think Red Clarkson started that fire?" Sam asked, frightened.

"He seemed to be ready to kill me in the dream I was having," Tad said. "He's gone from trying to scare us to trying to kill us."

He held up his hands. "And don't *you* start telling me about my imagination. This wasn't an everyday nightmare. It's as if I were awake, but I was still dreaming. The picture of Johnny Bodine in the saloon came alive. Johnny was trying to talk to me, but I couldn't hear him. All I know is that he was trying to tell me something about the key."

Tad took out the key that Johnny Bodine had tossed to him. "Somehow this whole thing has something to do with this key," he said.

He told Sam everything that happened in the dream. "Then Red Clarkson came into the dream, and I woke up. The next thing I knew, the hay was going up in smoke."

Tad studied the key, still in his palm. He frowned at the mysterious letters cut into the key's shaft, *AHTA-WAIH*. "If Bodine was trying to tell me what that message was, I didn't understand him."

He lay back. His throat felt sore from inhaling the smoke, and his muscles ached from pushing against the door. "We ought to try to get some sleep. After all, there'll be a lot of searching to do tomorrow."

"You're right," Sam admitted. "Well, have a good night, Tad."

"Same to you."

It seemed that Tad had just closed his eyes when once again he was walking through the doors of the Last Chance Saloon. Tad walked to where the misty wall waited for him. He passed the picture of the woman in red, passed the warrior . . .

Johnny Bodine was leaning out of the frame of his picture. He pointed again to the wall behind the bar. Tad saw himself and the other pictures reflected in the mirror.

The outlaw seemed to be pointing to one of the pictures in the mirror. Tad gazed at the pictures' reflections.

His jaw dropped as he realized what he was seeing. Digging into his pocket, he pulled out the key. "What a sneaky trick," he said. "What a sneaky trick."

Tad woke up to find himself laughing. He dug the key out of his pocket. After carefully examining the letters cut into the metal, he chuckled again. The letters worked out. The whole thing made sense!

Quietly Tad got out of his blankets and crept over to where Sam lay. She was sound asleep.

"Sam," he whispered.

She mumbled and turned away.

"Wake up," Tad said more insistently. "Come on, Sam. Listen to me. Believe it or not, I think I've figured out where the key goes!"

Chapter 10

"HUH? Whuzzat?" Sam mumbled as Tad shook her awake. She blinked blearily at Tad. "Juzwentzleep," she complained.

Then her eyes opened wide, and she looked around almost fearfully. "Tad!" Sam whispered. "What is it? Not more ghosts—"

"No ghosts," Tad cut her off. "I finally understood the message on the key—with a lot of help from Johnny Bodine."

"But we couldn't make any sense out of those letters," said Sam. "I saw you trying to make them into other words. It didn't work."

"We were wrong," Tad told her. "I think those letters tell us where to find the lock that goes with the key. I'm going to check it out right now." He somehow felt there was no time to lose. "Want to come with me?"

Sam immediately began getting up. "Are you kidding? Of course I'll come!"

Beyond the glow of dying embers from the fire, everything was dark. There was no moon to light their way.

"We'll need a light," Sam whispered, rummaging in her pack.

A second later she had a small flashlight in her hand. She flicked it on and said, "You never know when one of these will come in handy. Okay, let's go."

They set out along Kittredge's silent main street. Except for Sam's small light shining in front of them, it was almost pitch-black. Tad could barely make out the shape of the old buildings on either side of them. The only sound was the thump of their footsteps on the packed dirt.

Then, from the distance, came the mournful howl of a coyote. Tad and Sam both stopped dead in their tracks, their heads swiveling toward the sound. They turned to each other with embarrassed grins.

"Come on," Tad said. "Let's get this over with. I can't take all this excitement much longer."

They reached the Last Chance Saloon and entered. Sam's flashlight threw a dim pool of radiance as she aimed the beam on the barroom floor.

"You're sure the secret is in here?" Sam said, her voice skeptical. "How come we didn't see it when we were in here before?"

"We did," Tad told her. "The problem is, we just didn't realize it."

Taking Sam's hand, he led her to the huge mirror behind the bar. "We tried to find a code, to find scrambled words. But we never noticed the letters themselves."

"What were we supposed to notice?" Sam asked.

"If you hold these letters up to a mirror, they spell out a different word," Tad explained.

Slipping the strange key out of his pocket, Tad held it up to the barroom mirror. "See?"

Sam aimed the light at the reflection. "Now they spell *HIAWATHA*. But what—"

Tad took the flashlight from her hand and aimed it at the far wall—at the middle picture. There was the old print, the romantic picture of the warrior. Underneath was the name, *Hiawatha*.

Sam gasped. "Tad, you're a genius!"

Together they rushed across the room. As Tad held the flashlight, Sam lifted the picture frame off its nail. She snatched the flashlight back from Tad and turned it on the back of the picture.

"Nothing," she said, disappointment in her voice. "I guess you were wrong. There's no message here, no map, no place to go to use that key."

"Or *is* there?" Tad suddenly said. He took the flashlight and aimed it at the wooden wall where the picture had hung.

It was easy to tell the old picture's place. There was a neat rectangle of dark wood, the spot where the bleaching rays of the sun had never reached. In the middle of the spot, right under the nail supporting the picture, was a glint of metal.

"It's a keyhole!" Sam whispered excitedly. She took the flashlight from Tad while he reached up with the key. For a second he fumbled. Then the key slipped in.

Tad tried to turn the key, but the old lock resisted. Tad frowned. After all this, could he be wrong? Could this be the wrong key? He gritted his teeth and twisted as hard as he could. It was quite a struggle, but finally the lock gave a screech and clicked open.

The key popped back out of the lock. Sam and Tad stared eagerly. Nothing happened.

They both felt along the wall, pushing at various places, pounding against it.

"Hey," said Sam. "There's a thin line in the middle of this panel." She ran her fingers over a crack she had found in the wall.

Tad felt against the wall. The crack seemed to run from the floor to the ceiling. They put their hands to the wood beside the crack and pushed with all their might. For a second nothing happened. Then the wood creaked, gave a little, stuck again—and suddenly swung in. It was a door!

Tad and Sam stumbled forward, then jumped back, sneezing from the musty, cool air. They shone the flashlight over the small space. Inside the secret space was a hole leading deep into the ground. The shaft had a wooden ladder built into one side.

"Tad," Sam said, "what *is* this?"

"A secret mine?" Tad said, excited. "Or maybe it's a getaway tunnel, or the entrance to a secret room!"

He licked his lips, which had suddenly become dry. "Who knows what we'd find down there? Buried bodies—or maybe a treasure."

"There's only one way to find out," Sam said, handing him the flashlight. "We're going down."

Tad held the light on the ladder rungs as Sam climbed down. "I've reached bottom," she announced, her face gleaming in the light as she looked up. "It's maybe eight feet deep. Pass the light down—careful!" she said as Tad leaned into the shaft. "Now I'll light your way."

In a moment they were together again, peering with the help of the flashlight into a tunnel driven back through the ground.

The underground passageway had been crudely dug, with rough dirt walls. It was high enough for Tad to stand up in, though. Thick wooden beams placed every few feet supported the roof of the tunnel. It was crooked, and reminded Tad of the throat of a giant snake. Sam gulped nervously. Tad couldn't believe they had actually discovered a secret tunnel. The flashlight beam petered out into darkness. They couldn't see an end to the passage.

Tad frowned. "I don't get it," he finally said. "I thought maybe this might be a hiding place or it might lead to a hidden exit to the building next door. But as far as I can figure, this tunnel is leading out under the street."

He strained his eyes, squinting into the darkness. "*Way* out under the street."

"Well, we won't find what's at the other end unless we start walking," Sam said, eager to explore. She played the flashlight down the passage, peeking behind the first set of supports. "It looks solid enough. And nothing nasty seems to be hiding. No skulls or scorpions."

She sneezed. "Just a lot of dirt." Sam shivered a little. "And it's a lot colder down here than up in the saloon."

"I guess that's what happens when you have several feet of dirt between you and the sun," Tad said. He moved after Sam, starting down the tunnel.

They had only gone a few yards when Tad glanced back at the ladder.

"Hey!" Tad said. "There's a light on in the barroom!"

Sam turned in surprise.

Tad was right. A dim light was coming from above the hole, lighting up the bottom of the shaft.

"I'm going back to check it out," Tad whispered.

He went back and leaned out from behind the first set of wooden supports to peek up the shaft.

A wave of freezing air hit him, but that wasn't why his blood went cold.

The light in the old saloon didn't come from a

lamp, a flashlight, or a candle. It wasn't a natural light at all.

The weird radiance came from a figure that was glaring down into the shaft.

It came from the pale skin and flashing eyes of Red Clarkson!

Chapter 11

FOR a second that felt as if it would last forever, Tad stood frozen in fear. He was caught in Red Clarkson's glare like a small bird hypnotized by a snake.

Tad finally managed to tear words from a throat that had suddenly gone numb. "Sam! Run!" he croaked.

Even as Tad cried his warning, Red Clarkson began to move. The glowing ghost didn't need to take the ladder. Clarkson just stepped into the shaftway and slowly floated down. All the while he kept his awful eyes on Tad Miller.

Tad took a deep breath and whipped around to bolt down the tunnel.

"Run, Sam!" Tad yelled. "It's Red Clarkson. He's after us!"

Tad blundered along the crooked underground passage following Sam and her light. His arms scraped along the slimy dirt walls. He didn't know if it was possible to outrun a ghost. He knew he had no choice but to try. They had to get out of there!

He ran as fast as he could. Freezing air swirled around him.

Any second Tad expected icy fingers to clutch at him and drag him down. He didn't look forward to facing Red Clarkson's glowing eyes again. He pounded along the tunnel, his boots thudding on the hard-packed earth under his feet.

Then everything went dark. Tad slowed down and felt his way through the blackness. The tunnel must have curved, which was why he couldn't see Sam's light. He rounded a corner and was relieved to see the beam up ahead again. Then Tad realized that neither she nor the light were moving.

They had stopped, trapped by a large, iron-studded door!

"It's locked," Sam gasped. "We can't get through. We're trapped here! Clarkson's going to get us!"

As Tad came up, he saw that the door had no knob or handle. Instead, there was just a keyhole where the knob should be.

A keyhole!

Maybe it was a crazy hope, but it was the only one that he and Sam had. Tad dug into his pocket, tearing out his key again. He jammed it into the hole. It fit!

The lock clicked under his hand, and he and Sam pushed with everything they had. Slowly the massive door swung in on creaking hinges. As soon as there was enough space to get through, they jumped in past the door, then pushed it shut.

Sam's flashlight showed another keyhole on the door's other side.

Tad quickly locked the door and stepped back.

"Will that be enough to stop Clarkson?" Sam asked in a worried whisper.

"I—I don't know," Tad admitted. What could hold off an angry ghost?

Their voices seemed to echo more. As Sam turned and shone her light on the area, Tad could see why. On this side of the door the tunnel spread out to form a large chamber. The walls were reddish brown packed earth, but the ceiling was wooden planks. They were stained with dirt that had sifted through the spaces between boards.

Shadows cast by Sam's flashlight beam danced on the walls. She aimed it at the ground—and Tad gasped. The beam shone on a box in the middle of the chamber. It was about two feet wide, three feet long, and maybe a foot high. Stout metal straps surrounded the wooden side and top of the box. As Sam's light flashed on it, Tad could make out painted letters.

"Western Central Railroad," Sam read aloud. "That's an old railroad strongbox! What's it doing . . ."

Her voice faded away as both she and Tad realized what they were seeing.

"This must be the box that was stolen from the Cannonball," Tad whispered hoarsely. "The box that was stolen when Zeb Frobisher was shot dead." He ran to the center of the room, and stared at the dusty old chest. "This is the reason Johnny Bodine was arrested and hanged."

"I-is that why Johnny threw us the key?" Sam asked, her green eyes widening. "Do you think he wanted us to find his loot?"

"But *is* it Johnny Bodine's loot?" Tad asked, frowning. "Johnny threw us Red Clarkson's key. Remember? Marshal Clarkson was wearing it at Johnny's hanging. Johnny tore the key from around his neck."

He glanced at the door, still locked behind them. He hoped that the ghost couldn't come through the door. "And this secret passage began in Red Clarkson's barroom. Remember what Pete Stone told us? He was a part owner of the Last Chance Saloon," Tad explained.

Sam looked puzzled. "You're saying this doesn't belong to Johnny Bodine?" she said.

Tad didn't answer. He dropped to his knees beside the strongbox. This close up he could see a shining groove in one of the iron straps. That had to be the scar of a bullet, the bullet used to blast the lock away, he realized.

The box was unlocked. Tad pushed the top of the chest up. Behind him he could hear Sam's gasp as her flashlight beam glittered off hundreds, maybe thousands, of coins.

Tad saw big silver dollars, nickel-size gold pieces,

even huge twenty-dollar gold double eagles, all jumbled together. "It's a fortune," Tad exclaimed. He knew that collectors paid a lot of money for old coins. *What would these be worth in today's money?* Tad wondered, picking up one of the gold coins.

A bad taste filled his mouth. It didn't matter how much money this treasure might be worth. These coins were far too expensive. There was blood all over it. It had already cost the lives of two men—Zeb Frobisher and Johnny Bodine.

Tad frowned. There was something half-hidden among the shining coins. It was yellow, but didn't gleam. He dug down into the heaped treasure, sending the money rolling and clinking.

Slowly he drew out what had been mostly covered. Tad stared. It was a yellow bandanna with a black pattern.

He pulled out the bandanna he'd kept in his back pocket. He set it down next to the other one. Side by side, they were almost identical—*almost*. The yellow color was the same, but the designs on one were slightly smaller.

Yes. It all made sense now, Tad thought.

Then Sam screamed.

Tad leaped to his feet, turning to face the door. The ghost of Red Clarkson was floating through the iron-bound door! They could see Clarkson's figure, but it was like a cloud of mist.

The marshal seemed to ooze through the solid wood

and metal. His face looked like death itself as he glared at Tad and Samantha.

Sam shrank back until she was stopped by one of the posts holding up the ceiling.

Tad, however, squared off against the ghost. "This is some treasure you've got hidden down here, Marshal Clarkson," he said, sounding more confident than he felt. "But that strongbox shows how you got it. In fact, we know all about you now—all about what you did."

Now Clarkson was through the door, and solid again. He glared at Tad Miller, but didn't move. There wasn't just anger in the marshal's eyes. Tad thought he saw fear—and even shame.

"We heard some of the old stories about Johnny Bodine," Tad said, forcing himself to stare at the ghost. "He acted like Robin Hood. People helped him. You tried to catch Johnny and wound up looking foolish. Then you figured out a way to turn Johnny from a hero into a hated villain."

From behind him Sam whispered, "What are you talking about?"

Keeping his eye on Clarkson, Tad held out the two bandannas so Sam could see them. Sam gasped, and Red Clarkson's ghost actually took a step back. "This bandanna was in Clarkson's box," Tad said. "And there's only one reason to find it there. Red Clarkson dressed up as Johnny Bodine, stopped the Cannonball, and stole the money shipment."

Sam forgot her fear and stepped toward the ghost,

fury all over her face. "*You* shot Zeb Frobisher, even though he had no gun. You did it so people would turn against Zeb's killer—and they thought he was Johnny Bodine."

She was so angry, she was shaking. "You couldn't even stand up to Johnny in a fair fight!" she shouted. "We saw the third man backing you up from the Last Chance Saloon. He aimed before either of you drew. That was how you won the big gunfight. You made yourself famous by ruining Johnny Bodine's life!"

Sam snatched up handfuls of coins and began pelting them at the ghost. "You're no hero, Red Clarkson," she screamed. "You're a liar, thief, and killer. You're worse than Johnny Bodine ever was!"

Chapter 12

TAD stared in surprise. Red Clarkson actually stepped back from the coins Sam threw—even though the money passed right through him.

"Now we know why you were after us all this time," Sam yelled. "You didn't want us to find out the truth about you." She hurled another handful of coins. "But now we know your dirty secret, how you framed my great-great-granduncle and hanged him."

"Since you were related to Johnny Bodine, I guess Marshal Clarkson thought you'd be looking harder for the treasure," Tad said. "I'll bet that's why Johnny's been helping us, too."

"Well, now we'll be able to help *Johnny*," Sam declared. "We'll let the world know what a creep Red Clarkson really was. We'll clear Johnny's name!"

Red Clarkson stared straight at Sam. His eyes still

burned with shame, but he had obviously come to a decision—a grim decision.

"Sam," Tad said nervously as the ghost started toward them.

His friend was too busy throwing another fistful of coins at the ghost. Tad grabbed Sam's arm, and they started to retreat as Red Clarkson limped forward.

"We'll tell everyone what a lousy—" Sam continued to yell.

"Sam!" Tad hissed. "We're not going to tell anybody anything unless we get away from this guy."

Sam snapped out of her fury as she saw Red Clarkson reaching for his guns. "I—I think you're right, Tad," she said shakily. "Duck!"

They sprang apart as the ghost whipped out his guns and started shooting. Sam jumped behind one of the big, thick beams holding up the ceiling. Tad dropped the bandannas and dove for cover behind the opened strongbox. He saw the bullets, but again the gun made no sound. He didn't know whether the ghostly bullets could harm them, but he didn't dare to find out.

All of a sudden, the air around him felt very cold. He glanced up. A fancy cowboy boot was taking shape beside his right hand. The boot ran up to a black-clad leg. Then Tad saw a pair of six-guns, and over them, the face of Johnny Bodine.

A ghostly glow came from Johnny, but he seemed friendly as he gave Tad his usual half smile. Then the gunman opened fire, forcing Red Clarkson behind one of the roof supports. Bodine seemed to be enjoying the gunfight with Red Clarkson.

Then, while still firing one gun at the marshal, Johnny suddenly began pointing off to the right with his other pistol.

Tad stared in that direction. Was it his imagination, or was there an opening in the darkness among the shadows on that wall?

"Sam!" Tad called. "I think we have another way out of here. Can you get over to me?"

"I can sure try," Sam said. She waited for a lull in the shooting, then popped from behind the wooden post she'd been using for cover. Sam ran to another thick wood beam, then dove for another.

The problem was, she was still carrying the lit flashlight. It offered a ready-made target, and Clarkson turned, aiming carefully as she began her final run to get to Tad.

"Sam! Duck!" Tad yelled, watching the gun go off.

His friend dove, then screamed. As Sam hit the floor, the flashlight spun from her hand, to lie flickering on the floor.

"Sam, are you okay?" Tad shouted. He was sure she'd been hit by a bullet.

"He missed me," Sam said, "but I dropped the flashlight."

The small flashlight flickered madly, its light fading. Before it went out completely, Tad got a good look at the other exit from the hidden room. It was a large doorway like the one they'd come in—and the door was open.

A chill ran through Tad's body as an icy finger touched his shoulder. Johnny Bodine was trying to get his attention. Tad turned to the ghost. Johnny nodded toward Red Clarkson, then raised both his pistols.

"He's going to cover us while we run for the door," Tad said to Sam. "Are you ready?"

"I can't think of anything I'd like better than getting out of here," Sam admitted.

Tad had to smile. "That makes two of us. So let's try it—now!"

They burst from their hiding places as Johnny Bodine shot at his old enemy.

Together, Sam and Tad flung themselves through the opening and slammed the door behind them. Now they were safe from any wild shots. But without the eerie glow from the two ghosts, they had to stumble along in the dark.

The kids tried to move as quickly as they could, which wasn't easy in pitch-blackness. They felt their way forward carefully. This tunnel followed a crooked route, which made the going slow. They'd walk a few steps, and then the passage would veer off at some strange angle. Tad and Sam were constantly banging into support beams and dirt walls as they blindly groped their way along.

Sam's voice came out of the darkness. "Do you think we're safe? Are they coming after us?"

Tad's heart was beating so fast, he found it hard to talk. "I think we're okay, but who knows?"

"So now we know the terrible secrets that kept the ghosts here," Sam said. "Johnny Bodine wants to clear his name. And Red Clarkson wants to stop that from happening. There's just one thing I don't understand."

"What's that?" Tad asked, feeling his way in the tunnel's darkness.

"*Why?*" said Sam.

"Why what?"

"Why did Red Clarkson do what he did? I mean, he and Johnny were friends." Sam sighed. "What made him change so much that he had to ruin his friend's good name, then kill him?"

"Plain old jealousy, I guess. Let's hurry and get out of here. We can talk later. This place is giving me the creeps."

"Good idea," Sam said. The air was damp, and the darkness made it seem as if they were wearing blind-folds. Tad kept his hands out in front of him, feeling for pillars and dirt walls.

Suddenly Sam gasped and let out a cry of surprise.

Ahead of them was a flickering light! After wandering in complete blackness, the dim glow was blinding.

"Who's there?" a weak voice cried.

Sam grabbed Tad's hand. They recognized the voice bouncing off the packed dirt walls of the passageway.

Mr. Taylor was somewhere ahead of them!

Chapter 13

THE two friends moved more quickly toward the faint light up ahead in the passage. "Mr. Taylor!" Sam called. "Is that really you?"

The flickering light showed them the twists and turns of the passage. Sam and Tad ducked under a heavy beam holding up the ceiling, and turned another corner in the crooked underground pathway. They found themselves in a wider underground space.

Their teacher sat on the ground. The light they'd been seeing came from a tiny flame dancing at the end of a long wooden match he held.

"Samantha! Tad! So I wasn't imagining things! I *did* hear your voices."

Their teacher sounded happy to see them, but Tad didn't think Mr. Taylor looked very well. He sat hunched on the floor, his left leg held out very stiffly before him. The ankle was swollen and was twisted at an odd angle.

The skin on Mr. Taylor's face was pulled tight with strain. Deep lines creased his skin. He looked so pale and drawn that Tad found himself thinking of skulls as he stared at his teacher.

Mr. Taylor saw the concern on his students' faces.

"Are you okay?" Tad asked anxiously.

"I've had a bit of an accident," Mr. Taylor said, but he waved that away. "Right now I want to know what's going on up in the town. Are the other kids all right? I've been very worried. It's been a day since I fell down here."

"We're doing fine, so far," Tad told him.

"How did you get in here?" Sam asked.

"You might say I dropped in." Mr. Taylor said. Suddenly he winced in pain, his face going even paler.

Tad and Sam were on their knees in an instant, leaning over their teacher.

"How bad is it?" Tad asked anxiously. "Where does it hurt?"

"It's my ankle." Mr. Taylor whispered. He had his eyes closed, and sweat beaded on his brow. "I think it's broken. You know that I went out to check if anyone else was lurking around this town after the horses were stirred up."

He took a long breath and lit another match. "I thought I heard something in the old jailhouse, off in the back of the building. When I went to look in one of the cells, the floor gave out from under me. I remember falling, and that's about it. I must have hit my head or something. When I woke up, I could hardly move. I must have landed badly, otherwise I could have climbed right out."

Mr. Taylor extended his hand with the flickering match toward the wall behind him. A wooden ladder built into the wall extended up to a ragged hole in the ceiling above them. It was just like the ladder they'd used to climb down from the Last Chance Saloon.

"I don't quite understand what this tunnel is doing here," Mr. Taylor said. "But whoever dug it under the cell left it in the worst possible position for me. I spent hours yelling for help, but I guess no one heard my calls." Mr. Taylor lit another match as the other one burned down.

"We did search for you," Tad assured their teacher. "The cell you fell through must be in the very back of the jailhouse. Maybe no one checked all the way back there."

Mr. Taylor nodded. "I never heard anyone. But then, I may have been out cold when they came looking."

He held up a wristwatch with a shattered face. "I have no idea how much time has passed. My watch got broken in the fall. So did my flashlight."

Tad shuddered. All the time Mr. Taylor had been gone, he'd been trapped there. He couldn't move. He couldn't even tell how much time had passed.

"Aren't you starving?" Sam asked.

"No, luckily I had my pack with some emergency supplies and a canteen of water," Mr. Taylor said.

Their teacher shook his head again, then cast a sharp eye at Sam and Tad. "How's the group? Is Pete Stone taking care of everyone? And what are you two doing down here?"

"When you disappeared, we went to get Pete Stone. But he wasn't around, either," Sam reported. "The kids are doing well enough. But I have to tell you, some of them are pretty scared."

Mr. Taylor frowned. "Pete wasn't around? That's odd. So you've been on your own."

Tad nodded. "We checked Pete Stone's place. There's no telephone or radio, so we couldn't contact anybody to call for help. We talked about sending a messenger out, but when we voted on it, we decided to stay here."

Now it was Mr. Taylor's turn to nod. "That was the right decision. Lee will be along soon enough to collect us." The teacher looked at them carefully. "No other problems?"

"Nothing much," Tad assured him.

Mr. Taylor spoke softly, lighting another match as the other one burned down. "This is my last match," he announced, giving them a searching glance. "How did you two find this tunnel? What are you doing here?"

Tad and Sam quickly explained about the key.

"When we took down the picture of Hiawatha in the Last Chance Saloon, we found a keyhole," Sam said. "When Tad unlocked it, we managed to open a secret panel."

She rushed on to tell about the discovery of the hidden treasure, and how Johnny Bodine's name could be cleared.

Tad noticed, however, that Sam did *not* mention ghosts. When he thought she was about to, Tad was surprised to see Sam dart a nervous glance down the dark tunnel.

Mr. Taylor was very excited at their discovery, so excited he didn't even ask some obvious questions about why they didn't have a light. "This could be a most exciting contribution to our local history," the teacher said. "I'd like very much to see this secret room—"

He winced and looked down at his ankle. "Once I'm up and on my feet again."

"But first we have to get you out of here," said Tad. He glanced doubtfully at the ladder. "I don't think there's any way the two of us can help you up that thing."

"Sure we can, if we get a rope and all the kids," Sam said. "We'll set up a hitch around Mr. Taylor's chest, then haul him up carefully."

Tad moved to the ladder. "Don't worry," he said. "We'll be back with help before you know it."

He reached the top rungs of the ladder while there was still a little light coming from below. "You stepped on some rotten wood up here and broke through."

Tad pulled himself up onto solid flooring. A second later Sam had joined him. They carefully moved around the broken trapdoor. As they did, the light from below went out.

"Don't worry, Mr. Taylor," Tad called down. "We'll be back right away with help."

"I know." The teacher's voice floated up from the darkness. "You know where to find me. Where else am I going?" He gave a dry little chuckle.

Tad and Sam felt their way out of the cell. The place was built solidly. Except for the iron bars, the walls of the cell were made of thick adobe mud bricks. Groping along them with one hand as he moved through the darkness, Tad almost felt as if he were in the tunnel again.

At last he found the bars, then the door, and then they were heading down a corridor to the marshal's office.

Sam's mind was already on the rescue operation. "I'm pretty sure Randy Moser brought a rope along," she said. "If not, well, Pete Stone is sure to have some rope around somewhere."

Tad groped his way through the sheriff's office. Not even starlight filtered through the dust-streaked windows. He opened the front door and stepped into the silent main street.

Sam stepped past him, starting down the street toward the livery stable. Tad started to follow but suddenly stopped.

"Hey!" Tad said. Sam glanced back over her shoulder. "What is it?" she asked.

"Don't you see it?" he asked, pointing across the street to the Last Chance Saloon.

There was a glow of light coming from the big barroom!

Chapter 14

"WHAT do you think *that* is?" Sam whispered to Tad, watching the gleam of light slowly fade. "I thought we were okay when Clarkson's ghost didn't chase us."

"It's not glowing the way Clarkson or Johnny Bodine did," Tad said.

"So you're saying the light isn't ghosts," Sam said.

"That's right. Let's check it out." Tad started across the street. Sam followed beside him.

They entered the saloon, but the big barroom was empty. None of the old oil lamps were lit. There was no ghostly radiance.

The telltale glow was coming from the secret panel, which was still open. Tad saw that the light was growing a little fainter with each second.

"Somebody's carrying a light down the ladder!" Tad

exclaimed. He and Sam rushed to the secret entrance. As they reached the top of the ladder, the mysterious light bearer had already reached the bottom and disappeared into the tunnel.

It took only a second's glance for the two kids to decide what to do. Sam climbed down the ladder, followed by Tad.

They followed the glow of light along the twisting course of the underground passage, but couldn't see its source. Ahead of them, they heard the clashing sounds of metal against metal, then a loud creaking noise.

As they rounded the curve that led to the secret room, they saw a light coming from inside. The door was open. Its lock had been broken. Then they heard a loud gasp from inside—and the jingling of coins.

Tad and Sam stepped through the doorway and into the glow of an old-fashioned lantern. The lamp was set beside the Western Central Railroad strongbox. Kneeling in front of the box, his back to them, was Pete Stone. His arms were plunged up to the elbows in gold coins, and he was chuckling to himself.

"Pete!" Tad called.

The bearded man twisted around, glaring over his shoulder at them. Greed shone in his eyes, and his lips were twisted in a gloating smile.

"You kids following me?" he demanded. Then he shook his head. "No, no. I was following you. Ever since you showed me that key, I knew you were searching for Johnny Bodine's treasure."

"It's not Johnny Bodine's treasure," Sam said. "It's Red Clarkson's. He's the one who stole—"

"Who cares!" Stone cut her off. "This is the loot from the great Cannonball robbery, and I found it!" He eyed them angrily. "Do you know how many years I've spent in this stinking town, looking for this gold? It was a heck of a life, just me, the snakes, and the spiders. I searched all the buildings, dug pits near every landmark, and wound up with nothing."

Pete Stone let the gold coins dribble between his fingers and shifted around to face them. "Of course, I always had to keep an eye on whoever came to town. Had to make sure they weren't going after my treasure. They all thought I was just good old Pete, mayor of Kittredge. But I kept close to them all. They weren't going to steal this out from under my nose!"

Stone smiled craftily. "Then you kids came. I heard about you," he said, pointing at Sam. "One of the kids told me you were Johnny Bodine's niece."

"Great-great-grandniece," Sam said.

"It doesn't matter," the bearded man said, plunging his hands into the golden coins. "I knew you were here for the treasure," he accused. "You had hardly arrived before you were poking around, sneaking away from the others."

Pete Stone frowned. "I even saw you upstairs in the old saloon. Should have realized right then that you had a clue about where the treasure was. Instead, I let you take me in with those silly ghost stories."

Tad blinked. "You mean you've never seen any ghosts around Kittredge?"

"I didn't come here looking for ghosts," Stone yelled. "I came here looking for gold!" A sly look came over his face. "I knew you wouldn't really go after the treasure if you thought I was around. So I pretended to leave town. I hid while you and the other kids went searching for me. Then I kept an eye on the livery stable, because I knew, sooner or later, you two would come on out."

Tad could feel his face heating with anger. "You mean, you heard us looking for Mr. Taylor, and you wouldn't help search for him?"

Sam was even angrier. "You saw us trapped in the livery stable with a fire going, and you didn't try to get us out?"

Pete Stone just shook his head. "You weren't going to fool me into showing myself."

An icy cold shiver went down Tad's back. He and Sam had faced visions and ghosts in the last few days, and come through fine. Now it dawned on him that they were in more danger from a live man—a man who had gone crazy in his long search for the Cannonball treasure.

Stone was still shaking his head. "Sure enough, you finally came out. Who would have thought of a secret door hidden in the wall of the old saloon? And this room—" He looked up at the ceiling overhead. "I must have walked across this spot about a million times, crossing the street. And over all the years I never guessed the treasure was right under my feet."

He grabbed again for the golden coins. "But I've got it now!" Stone glared at the two kids, suddenly fearful. "But if I followed you here, how'd you get behind me?"

Sam pointed to the open door on the far side of the room. "Red Clarkson dug another tunnel. It runs across the street to the jailhouse."

Ted nudged Sam, hoping she wouldn't say more, but she kept on going.

"Mr. Taylor is trapped down there. He fell through the floor and broke his ankle. We have to get him out," Sam finished.

Pete Stone stared at her, his dark eyes glinting. "So Taylor is trapped down here, and you kids are out alone, are you?"

Tad really wished that Sam hadn't told Stone anything.

He felt even worse when the bearded man abruptly turned from the strongbox and snatched up an old pickax. The metal point of the digging tool was shiny and slightly bent. Stone had obviously used it to smash the lock off the door.

Pete Stone rose to his feet, gripping the handle of the pick in both hands.

"I deserve this gold," the bearded treasure seeker said angrily. "I've been looking for it for years. Who are you to come in and find it in a couple of days? It's not fair. You're not taking it away from me! You're not!" he roared, raising the pick and stepping grimly toward them.

Tad and Sam shrank back, but there was nowhere for them to go. Pete Stone was blocking the way to the other exit from the room. If they tried to run back down the other tunnel in the dark, he'd catch them before they reached the ladder back to the saloon.

"There's two of you and only one of me, but I'm bigger," Stone cackled. "All I have to do is put that secret panel back the way it should be. People will think you've simply disappeared—just like your precious Mr. Taylor."

The mad treasure seeker laughed. "That'll teach you for trying to steal my gold." Pete Stone raised the pickax over his head.

Tad suddenly stiffened, looking Stone right in the eye. "I don't think giving away this gold is up to us," he said. "You should talk to the man who guards the gold. He's right behind you."

Stone gave a loud guffaw. "You think I'm going to fall for that old trick?" he demanded. "Just for that, *you* get it first!"

The crazed prospector advanced on Tad, his pickax still raised high.

Then came the roar of a gunshot, deafening in the enclosed space. A bullet tore the digging tool right out of Stone's hands.

"Wha—?" babbled Pete Stone, turning around. Then he spun around in shock.

For the first time in his life, the honorary mayor of Kittredge was actually seeing one of the town's ghosts. It was a dark-clad figure with a yellow bandanna round its neck, a pair of six-guns in its hands, and a half smile on its face.

Johnny Bodine floated over the box full of coins, his pistols aimed at Pete Stone. For a long moment the bearded man stared at the ghost. Stone's eyes bugged out; his lips trembled under the heavy whiskers.

Then he started backing toward the door back to the Last Chance, his eyes only on the ghostly presence. Stone inched by Tad and Sam without a glance.

Johnny Bodine floated a step closer. With a terrified yell, Stone turned and bolted through the door. They could hear him bumping into the walls as he raced down the dark tunnel.

"Th-thanks," Tad managed, staring up at Johnny Bodine. Only now did Tad realize that the ghost's bullets had been real.

The ghostly gunfighter nodded and smiled.

"I'm glad somebody else besides us finally saw you," Sam said. She grinned as she glanced down the dark tunnel. "But I doubt if we'll see him again."

Tad watched as Johnny Bodine's figure started to dissolve.

"He's disappearing!" Sam cried.

Johnny Bodine was gone, but the foggy cloud he'd become remained. It swirled around them, so thick that it blotted out the light from Pete Stone's lantern. Tad shivered as the fog seemed to reach out and touch him. Not only was it dank, it was cold.

"W-what's going on?" Sam demanded, her teeth chattering.

The fog moved faster and faster around them, and a high-pitched, howling wind came at them.

"Tad!"

Sam was standing right beside him, clutching his arm, but he could hardly hear her.

The wind rose in a final shriek.

Then everything went black.

Chapter 15

THE wild wind tore at them, spinning even more violently around them. Tad couldn't see a thing, but he felt the breath being squeezed from his body.

I thought Johnny Bodine was our friend, he thought. *Is this the way it's going to end?*

"Tad!" Sam cried in terror. "What's going on? Why—"

Her voice rang out into sudden silence. The shrieking whirlwind that had attacked them so suddenly had just as suddenly stopped.

The fog still swirled crazily around the two friends, too thick for them to see through. Somehow, though, Tad had the feeling they were no longer in the underground chamber. He wasn't sure *why* he felt that way. Then he realized there was no echo when Sam yelled.

As the fog faded away, Tad saw he was right. He

and Sam now stood in front of the jailhouse, in the middle of Kittredge's main street. The building, and indeed the whole town, was very different.

No longer was Kittredge a ghost town. The windows of the jailhouse were clean and polished. The words *TOWN MARSHAL* gleamed on the door in shiny new gold paint. Even the humble adobe walls of the jailhouse were dazzling with a fresh coat of whitewash.

The signs over the other stores and buildings of the town were painted in bright reds and yellows, blues and greens.

Tad realized this was the way the town must have looked before a century of desert sun had faded all the colors to gray. Everything was brand-new. The very wood that made up the buildings seemed raw and fresh, as if it had been just sawed and hammered into shape.

This was Kittredge in its young and brawling past, as a new boomtown on the frontier.

"Everything in town is new," Sam said, staring around, trying to make sense of this. "Have we gone back in time? Why did Johnny take us here?"

"I don't know," Tad told her.

The street was now filled with men in cowboy boots and hats, and women in long dresses. The tinkle of old-time piano music drifted out from the Last Chance Saloon. Horse-drawn wagons rumbled down the dusty street, and the sweet smell of sarsaparilla wafted out of the saloon. No one noticed Sam or Ted. It was as if they were invisible.

Whenever Tad focused on anything too closely, he saw the same ghostly glow he had seen on Red Clarkson and Johnny Bodine. He noticed that the high-noon sun shone less brightly than the moon. It cast a weird half-light on the scene around them.

A pair of figures suddenly appeared on the bustling main street of town. One was short and wiry, dressed all in black except for the yellow bandanna he wore around his neck. The short figure tipped back his hat, a half smile on his cheerful young face.

"You know I didn't rob the Cannonball, Red," Johnny Bodine called to the other man. "And I didn't shoot Zeb Frobisher."

Marshal Red Clarkson wore a pair of dusty gray trousers, a white shirt, and a black vest with a star on it. He had no hat, and his long red hair was combed back.

His lips were a tight line under his red mustache. "That's what you say, Johnny. But I've got witnesses that say otherwise."

Clarkson stepped toward Johnny Bodine. Tad thought there was something different about the man—Red Clarkson wasn't limping. He was also amazed to realize that he could actually hear the men speak. "I've got to take you in, Johnny," Clarkson said.

The strange half smile still tugged at Johnny Bodine's lips. "Can't let you do that, Red."

They were now standing face-to-face. Johnny suddenly untied the bandanna from around his neck and held it in his left hand. "Might as well do this up close," he said. "Save the town any wild shooting."

He shook out the square of cloth, then held out his hand. "You take the other end. When you feel lucky, draw."

Sam and Tad stood spellbound, watching the duel unfold again. No one else in the town seemed to notice what was happening. Then Tad remembered the last time they'd seen this fight. He glanced over toward the doors of the Last Chance Saloon.

Sure enough, another ghostly hand had appeared, aiming a six-shooter at Johnny Bodine. Now Tad realized why Johnny had brought them here. He wanted someone to back him up at this fight!

"No!" Tad cried. "Not this time!"

He dashed across the street, ignoring Johnny and Red. All Tad's attention was on the hidden gunman, the man Red Clarkson had used to cheat Johnny Bodine out of a fair fight.

As he reached the doorway, Tad heard the flat click of the gun's hammer being pulled back.

Tad didn't glance back to see what the two gunfighters were doing. He plowed straight into the swinging door, sending it crashing back against the figure hiding inside. He heard the man cry out. Tad leaped inside and stared at the man. He had on an oversize shirt, with several scissors and a razor in the pocket. It was the Kittrdege barber!

At that moment, Tad heard a double roar as a pair of pistols went off.

He turned to see Johnny Bodine standing over Red

Clarkson. The marshal lay in the sandy main street. Strangely, he could see no anger in Red Clarkson's face. In fact, the only word he could use to describe the marshal's expression was peaceful.

Johnny Bodine wasn't smiling as he knelt beside his onetime friend. There was pity in his gaze.

"Well, Johnny," Red Clarkson said in a weak voice. "Back when we were friends, you'll remember I always was a gambling man. This time I gambled and lost— the way I should have lost all those years ago. Fair's fair. I done you a terrible wrong, and now I got to pay for it."

The ghostly marshal glanced over at Tad and Sam. "But these kids you brought along will clear your name. The world will know that Johnny Bodine never killed a man in his life."

Red Clarkson looked down at his mortal wound and actually managed a smile. "And killin' ghosts doesn't count."

Clarkson took in a deep, shuddering breath. "*Adiós, amigo,*" he whispered. "Remember the old days, the happy times we had on the trail together. I wish—"

They never found out what Red Clarkson wished. He shuddered for a second, and then was very still.

Johnny Bodine stared in silence as his old friend, his old enemy, passed away. Then he glanced at Tad and Sam, who had come from opposite sides of the street to join him.

"Is it finally over?" the young gunfighter said in a quiet voice. "After all this time?"

"We'll make sure everybody knows the real story," Sam promised fiercely.

Tad found himself grinning, but there was a question he had to ask. "There's just one thing I don't understand," he said to the ghostly gunman. "If you knew about Red Clarkson's secret room and the strongbox being there, why didn't you tell people at your trial?"

The odd smile returned to Johnny Bodine's face. "I *didn't* know back then," he said. "I kind of suspected Red. But he used to be my friend. And I had no proof he was the rider who'd hit the train. I only learned the whole story after I had passed over. And that was a little too late."

"Now we can clear you," Sam said. "Maybe it was a long time coming, but it will happen now."

Johnny Bodine gave them a tip of his broad-brimmed hat. Even as Johnny smiled at them, Tad realized that he could see through the ghostly gunman.

Red Clarkson's body had already dissolved into mist. All the buildings around them were also shimmering, as if they were pictures that had gone out of focus. The murky light around them swirled into nothingness.

Tad blinked. The ghosts were gone. He and Sam were standing in the middle of Kittredge's main street. The moon had finally risen, and Tad and Sam could see that once again, the wooden buildings were a century old and weather-beaten. Tad let out the long breath he'd been holding.

"Looks like we're back home," he said. "Or at least back in plain, normal Kittredge."

Sam nodded, breathing a sigh of relief. "No more ghosts, no more scary stuff. Now all we have to do is get the group and rescue Mr. Taylor."

"Fine," Tad said as they made their way down the street toward the livery stable. "Let's do it before anything else weird happens."

Chapter 16

THE other Chilleen students were still fast asleep when Tad and Sam returned to them. It wasn't easy to wake the sleepers, until they heard that the two had found Mr. Taylor.

"He's down in a hole?" Randy Moser said, rubbing sleep from his eyes.

"There's a tunnel that runs under the jailhouse," Sam explained. "Mr. Taylor went to look in one of the old cells, the floor gave way, and he fell in."

"How come we didn't find him then?" Jeff Dearborn demanded. "Who searched the jailhouse?"

Randy looked at the floor. "Jane and I were supposed to do it," he said, embarrassed. "It was right after she freaked when that big spider crawled out from under the general store. Jane stayed outside, and I took a quick look around. I only checked the office, and hardly glanced back at the cells."

"Well, we found Mr. Taylor now," Tad consoled. "And Sam says you may have a rope."

"I do," Randy said, anxious to help. "It's over here, hanging from my saddle."

With Randy's rope, a first aid kit, a couple of flashlights, and one of Pete Stone's kerosene lamps, the six kids set off for the jailhouse.

Mr. Taylor was very glad to see some light entering his black hole. "Sam? Tad? Is that you?"

"It's all of us," Tad called down. "We'll have you out of there pretty soon."

He turned to Randy. "I think you're the best at tying knots and loops. Can you rig something up to go around Mr. Taylor's chest and under his arms so we can pull him up?"

Then Tad asked the others if anyone knew first aid. "Before we move him, we really should get Mr. Taylor's ankle bandaged, or splinted, or something."

"I know a little about that sort of stuff, from gymnastics," Monica said. She and Randy climbed down the ladder. Monica wrapped the teacher's ankle, and then the others lowered the rope.

Getting Mr. Taylor out of the shaft wasn't as hard as Tad had feared. The teacher was able to balance himself on the ladder with his good leg while they hauled him up one rung at a time.

As soon as he was out of the hole, the first thing their

teacher wanted to see was the hidden loot from the Cannonball.

"You mean you also found Johnny Bodine's treasure?" Monica cried in disbelief.

"It looks as if we'll have to start calling it Red Clarkson's treasure," Mr. Taylor said. "Sam and Tad found the money in a room in the tunnel halfway between Clarkson's office and the saloon he owned."

Tad and Sam quickly told Mr. Taylor about Pete Stone and his threats. Mr. Taylor assured the kids that as soon as Lee arrived, he would have him alert the Phantom Valley sheriff. The teacher was positive that Stone would be caught.

Then, at Mr. Taylor's insistence, they left him resting in the marshal's office, lying comfortably on the floor with his injured leg up. The students took on the job of moving the heavy strongbox full of coins from the hidden room and up through the saloon.

"This is pretty cool," Monica said, examining the secret panel in the barroom. "That was a smart way to hide the keyhole." She smiled admiringly at Tad. "And you were pretty smart to figure out what the letters on the key meant."

The sky was beginning to go pale with the first light of dawn by the time they finally got the strongbox up and over to the marshal's office. Mr. Taylor's eyes lit up as he looked at the coins glittering in the light of the kerosene lamp.

"Amazing," he said.

"It's a real treasure," Jane said in an awed voice.

"Oh, this box is much more than that," the history teacher said, closing the strongbox to look at the railroad company's markings. "Tad and Sam have actually turned up a piece of our local history. Finding the lost Cannonball loot clears up the great mystery of where it went. But by finding the loot where they did, they have also saved the reputation of Johnny Bodine."

Monica nodded. "Now we know that whatever else Johnny Bodine may have done, he wasn't a murderer."

Sam's lips curved in a secret smile. "He may have been a badman, as they said in the old days," she whispered. "But he wasn't a *bad* badman."

"That's a very good way of putting it," Mr. Taylor said.

Tad accepted congratulations and backslapping from the other students on his discovery and the way they'd come through the adventure. As soon as he could, though, he stepped out onto the wooden sidewalk outside the marshal's office.

The sun was just rising over the hills to the east. It cast a rosy light over the whole valley. Tad just leaned against the hitching post, watching the light get brighter and brighter.

After a little while, Sam came out to join him. "Pretty, isn't it? It certainly turned out to be some trail ride," she said with a laugh. "How did you like your taste of the Old West?"

Tad grinned. "I sure didn't think I'd end up backing Johnny Bodine in a gunfight."

"Well," said Sam, "you proved that you'd have had what it took to be a pioneer."

Suddenly she stared and pointed. "What's that?"

"What's what?" Tad asked, looking down. Then he saw a scrap of yellow sticking out of his pocket. He tugged, and out came a square of patterned yellow cloth.

Tad stared. "The bandanna!" he gasped. "But I dropped both of them in the treasure room when Red Clarkson began banging away. I *know* I dropped them."

Sam frowned. "When we went back to pick up the strongbox, I didn't see either of them." She shook her head. "Looks like great-great-granduncle Johnny keeps up his jokes to the end."

Tad folded the bandanna in half, then tied the neckerchief around his throat. This time it didn't tighten up. It was a piece of cloth.

Jane stuck her head out the jailhouse door. "What are you two talking about out there?" she asked. Then her eyes went wide. "Wow! Cool bandanna. Where did you get it?"

Tad gave her a smile. "It's just a souvenir," he said. "A present from an old friend."

About the Author

LYNN BEACH was born in El Paso, Texas, and grew up in Tucson, Arizona. She is the author of many fiction and nonfiction books for adults and children.

Coming next—

Phantom Valley ™

IN THE MUMMY'S TOMB

Stephanie Markson puts on the Egyptian necklace her mother bought for her, and strange things quickly begin to happen. A mysterious black cat, with one green eye and one blue, menacingly stalks her around Chilleen. In her dreams, Stephanie is haunted by a dangerous cat woman. She's sure she hears the word *return* being uttered both by the cat and the cat woman. Now Stephanie and her two friends, Ben and Laura, must discover what the cat and cat woman want her to do, before she becomes the latest victim of an ancient Egyptian curse!